Murder on the Levels

by

Frances Evesham

An Exham on Sea Mystery

CHAPTER ONE

Forest Chocolates

The warm tang of yeast percolated through Exham on Sea's bakery. "This must be the quietest place on the planet." Libby Forest didn't mean to complain, but there hadn't been much excitement here, lately.

Frank, the baker, dumped a pair of disposable gloves in the kitchen bin, hoisted a crate of fresh loaves, grunted, and shuffled backwards through the door. "Time to revamp the bakery, then. Make some space for those hand-made *Forest Chocolates*." Libby's knife clattered to the table. Had she heard right?

Mandy, Exham on Sea's resident teenage Goth, pumped a tattooed arm. "Our very first proper chocolate shop."

A big fat grin forced its way across Libby's face. It was weeks since she'd presented her business plan. Frank had sucked his teeth, scratched an ear and mumbled, "We'll see." She'd almost given up

1

hope. Maybe it was the constant supply of free samples that wore him down.

His head bobbed back around the door. "Are you in a fit state to drive, Libby? The cycling club left their sandwiches in the van." He thrust packages into Libby's arms.

Mandy giggled. "Too busy stuffing themselves with free chocolates. Kevin Batty gobbled up at least three lemon meringue truffles."

Still in a daze, Libby loaded the sandwiches into her ancient purple Citroen, crunched the gears and drove out onto the Somerset Levels, following the cyclists' route through corkscrew lanes beneath a broad blue spring sky. Her head whirled with plans for packaging, marketing, future outlets and exotic new chocolate flavours. She turned up the CD player and bellowed *We Are The Champions* at the top of her voice. Why not? No one could hear it in this peaceful corner of the West Country.

The car squealed round a corner, narrowly avoiding a row of bicycles propped against a wooden fence. It lurched to a halt and Libby jumped out. Beyond an open gate, clumps of sedge and willow lined the placid waters of a stream. Moorhens ducked in and out of overhanging branches, and a pair of geese honked in the distance.

Libby slithered on the grass. Patches of mud, still damp from a brief overnight rainstorm, squelched under her feet. Not quite a country girl yet, then. She'd keep a pair of wellies in the car in future.

A hand grasped her elbow. "Careful." A few years older than Libby, Simon Logan had pleasing pepper and salt hair and a warm smile, and almost managed to make Lycra look elegant. As Mandy, Libby's lodger and self-appointed dating advisor, had pointed out, "He's divorced, no children, retired university lecturer, conductor of the local orchestra and much richer than Max Ramshore. He'll do for you, Mrs F."

Enjoying a sudden, welcome independence since her husband's heart attack ended their unsatisfactory marriage, Libby had scoffed at the idea. Intent on building a business and a new life, she didn't need male complications, thank you. Max Ramshore was hardly more than an acquaintance. She'd worked with the secretive ex-banker on Exham's recent celebrity murder investigation, but he'd left town without so much as a word.

"Lovely morning." Simon Logan's deep brown voice resonated pleasantly in Libby's ears, but she had no time to reply. Kevin Batty intervened, wiping streaks of sweat from sallow cheeks. His pointy-chinned, pink-eyed face lacked only a set of stiff whiskers to complete the resemblance to an over-friendly rodent.

He stood so close, Libby could count the pores on his nose. "Mrs Forest. Why don't you join us?" What's more, he'd been eating garlic.

About to refuse, Libby changed her mind when Simon joined the appeal. "The least we can do is offer you some of our lunch."

The heady smell of still-warm pastries made Libby's stomach growl. "Just an Eccles cake, then."

***

A smile still hovered over her face as she drove back to Exham. Mandy was taking the afternoon shift at the bakery, so Libby had the rest of the day free. She collected Shipley, a friendly, noisy springer spaniel, from her indolent friend Marina, and let him loose on the beach.

"Hi, Libby." Her sunny mood evaporated in a flash.

"Max."

"Still mad at me? How many times do I have to say I'm sorry? I had to leave town at short notice." Max threw a stick for his dog, Bear, the owner of four vast paws and the shaggiest coat Libby had ever seen. Bear loped steadily along the sand to fetch it, while Shipley raced back and forth, barking, ineffective, and wild with excitement.

Max didn't look sorry. In fact, he'd gained a light tan that made his Scandinavian eyes gleam brighter and his thick silver hair shimmer. He was grinning, expecting to be forgiven. Libby exaggerated her shrug. "It's quite all right. You don't have to tell me when you go away. Anyway, it wasn't you I missed. It was Bear."

Max threw the stick again. "I couldn't leave him with you. He's too big for your cottage, so I sent him off to have a little holiday with a farmer friend of mine."

"Well, I'm glad he's back." Of course, Max was right. Bear had stayed at her cottage before, and the carpets had never been the same, but Libby loved the giant animal more than home furnishings.

Max pulled a box from the pocket of his waxed jacket. "I brought you a present. A peace offering."

Libby narrowed her eyes, suspicious. "What is it?"

"OK, if you don't want it..."

"Of course I want it. I never refuse presents." Libby unfolded layers of tissue paper inside the little blue box. "A fridge magnet. How nice."

"Look what it says. *World's Greatest Cook*. That's you."

She tried not to laugh. "You think flattery will get you anywhere. My son gave me one just like it, years ago, when he was about twelve."

"I may be childish, but am I forgiven?"

Why be grumpy while the sun's shining? "Maybe. My book came out, by the way. *Baking at the Beach* is now available world-wide. I'm just waiting for my own copies to arrive."

"No. Really? Why didn't you tell me? Wait, because I wasn't here. Now I really do feel bad."

"Good. Then I forgive you."

"To make up, I'll buy your first hardback copy."

Libby snorted. "Can't imagine you baking cakes, somehow." She found a length of driftwood and called to the spaniel. "Shipley, here's a stick, just for you. Bear, leave it alone." She held the sheepdog back, fondling the giant ears.

They'd already wandered past the nine-legged lighthouse, where Libby had discovered Susie Bennett's body last year. Exham on Sea disappeared from view, hidden by sand dunes, as they rounded the bend. Max cleared his throat. "Libby, there's something I need to..." He broke off and rolled his eyes as his phone trilled. "Sorry."

He stiffened. "What? How many?" A sharp intake of breath. "I'll be there."

"What's the matter?"

"There's been an accident. The cycling club, out on the Levels."

That couldn't be right. Everyone was fine when Libby left. "What sort of accident? A road crash?"

"Apparently not."

"Then what? Wait." Max was already pounding back along the beach, dogs galloping behind. Libby followed, scrambling awkwardly across the sand. Panting, she struggled up the steps from the beach to the road.

Max threw open the door of his Land Rover to let the dogs pile in. "That was Claire, Joe's wife, on the phone. She's meeting us at the scene."

"Is it serious?"

"Claire doesn't know. They're out at the wildlife reserve."

Earlier, Libby had exchanged a distant, formal nod with Joe, Max's son, down on the Levels. Their relationship was tricky. A detective sergeant in the local police force, he had as little time for Libby as he had for his father.

***

An ambulance left as Max and Libby arrived at the river. "There he is." Joe lay on the grass, face chalk-white, eyes closed. A paramedic nearby saw

Max and came over, squatting beside Joe. "Looks like a touch of food poisoning, sir. Half the club have keeled over."

"Food poisoning? Could it cause all this?" Max waved a hand at a scene of disaster. A few hardy cyclists hadn't actually passed out, but lay with their backs propped against tree trunks, clutching silvery blankets and shivering. Over by the stream, Simon Logan bent double, wiping his mouth. Had everyone been poisoned? Libby's own stomach lurched and she swallowed saliva. The sandwiches? No, surely not...

The young paramedic struggled to her feet. "Poison is poison. We'll get people to hospital, then we'll know more."

The officer in charge, Chief Inspector Arnold, nodded to Max. "Sorry to see that lad of yours is involved, Max, but we need to treat this as a crime scene." He peered at Libby. "Ah, Mrs Forest. I gather most of the cyclists bought their sandwiches at Frank's bakery?"

The knot in Libby's stomach tightened. "Well—yes, they did." She licked dry lips. "I brought the food out here..."

Max broke in. "Don't say any more."

Libby gulped. "You mean..."

"Don't say anything that might incriminate you. Or the bakery."

Libby's breath caught in her throat. "Do I need a lawyer?"

The Chief Inspector's face was inscrutable. "We'll talk to you properly, later. There's no need to worry, Mrs Forest, until we find out exactly what happened here."

Libby shivered. "The people in the first ambulance. Are they OK?"

"I'm afraid not. Kevin Batty and Vince Lane are dead."

CHAPTER TWO

Eccles cake

A small Ford Fiesta screeched to a halt and a woman leapt out, brown hair flying wildly in the spring breeze. "Claire. Glad you're here." Max hugged his daughter-in-law, awkward, as though they rarely touched. He proffered a set of car keys to Libby. "Would you do me a favour and take the dogs back to Exham, in the Land Rover? Claire and I need to get to the hospital."

Libby scrambled into the car, found reverse and set off with a succession of kangaroo hops. She wriggled, uncomfortable. Her trousers seemed to be too tight. She undid a button and laid one hand on her bloated stomach.

Her head was swimming, but she had to get back to the bakery to warn Frank about the food poisoning. Or, maybe she should go to the police station? It was so hard to think. Her cheeks burned. Beads of sweat broke out on her forehead and the stomach pain stabbed, knife-sharp. Libby slammed on the brakes, heaved open the door and fell out, just in time to throw up with long, painful gasps against the wheels of the car.

She groaned, leaned against the car to counteract rubber legs, fumbled for a handkerchief and scrubbed at streaming eyes. Another wave of nausea engulfed her body. Finally, exhausted, every scrap of her stomach contents now decorating Max's previously shiny wheels, Libby sank down on the verge beside the road. She was only halfway home, but she couldn't drive like this. Maybe someone would come along in a minute, and offer her a lift?

The peace and quiet of rural Somerset had its disadvantages. No cars passed. Not even a bicycle appeared. Another wave of sickness came and went, leaving Libby even weaker. Too tired to sit, she lay on one side, tears of self-pity sliding down her face. Was she going to die, like the cyclists? This would be even worse, all on her own out here.

The dogs barked, furious at being left in the car, and Libby had an idea. If she let them out, maybe they'd run away and find help. She could get to the car if she moved slowly enough. She ground her teeth and, shaky, staggered upright, trying to keep her head steady. The walk to the car might as well have been a mile, over grass that waved and rippled. She'd never make it.

"Looks like you're another victim." Someone had an arm round her and relief flooded Libby's body. Maybe she wasn't going to die just yet.

She tried to focus through a yellow haze. "Max?" With Max supporting one side and Claire the other, Libby stumbled to the Land Rover. She collapsed back into the passenger seat, dimly aware Max was talking.

He didn't sound sympathetic at all, just furious. "Why didn't you tell me you were ill? You shouldn't have been driving. What were you thinking?" Libby gulped air. Talking was too difficult.

"Here." Max offered a bottle of water. "Just a sip."

Libby scrubbed a hand across her face. "What about Joe?"

"He's comfortable. Sick as a dog in hospital, but not in any danger. His heart rate's up, but the doctors say it's not serious. They just want to keep him in until it slows. We left him there to get some sleep."

Claire, apparently deciding Libby would survive, returned to her car, hooted, and drove off. Libby fought back another wave of nausea as Max studied her face, his eyes narrow. She could almost see him thinking. "Did you eat or drink anything with the cyclists?" Libby let her eyes close, and the sickness receded. Max shook her arm. "Come on, try to concentrate."

"No." A memory surfaced, and her eyes opened wide. "At least, just one bite from an Eccles cake. But there was nothing wrong with it. I should know. I made it myself." She shuddered. The very idea of pastry tightened the knot in her stomach. "I feel better now." That was a lie. She longed, more than anything, to crawl quietly into her own bed.

"We need to get you to the hospital. I want you checked out."

"You think I've been poisoned, too?"

He leaned over to fasten her seatbelt. "Pretty obvious, I'd say, but we'll find out for sure."

Libby lay back, the chaos in her stomach subsiding. "I only had one small bite."

"Just as well. Luckily, Joe only ate half a sandwich."

"Poor Joe."

"I thought you didn't care for him."

Libby grunted. "Well, of course I care. He's your son, after all, and..." Exhausted, still nauseous, she couldn't think of the right words. She let the sentence tail off, too weak to follow through. "You know what I mean."

"He's prickly, that's the trouble with Joe. And a policeman, which makes it worse."

They drove in silence. Libby felt better, so long as she kept both eyes fixed on the road ahead. "I don't want to go to hospital."

"Too bad."

She tried again. "I was on my way to the police station. I want to find out what happened."

Max snorted. "Did you think the police would tell you anything?"

"Probably not. They think I'm a busybody."

"I'd call you interested and inquisitive. Can't blame them, really, after the Susie Bennett affair."

"It wasn't my fault the police didn't take her death seriously. Come on, Max. You were in it with me. You found out all sorts of things from your strange foreign contacts."

Several seconds ticked by before he answered. "Libby, you're talking about my other—er—responsibilities. You know I try to keep my distance from police work in Exham."

"Yes, I know. You have very secret and important work for the government. I found out about it, remember?" It hadn't been too difficult. All the signs had been there. Early retirement from high-level banking, regular sudden trips abroad, half-hidden links with the police, and easy access to foreign authorities. Everything pointed to a secret life. Max had to have been either a criminal or a government employee. Libby assumed she'd guessed right.

"Keep it to yourself, there's a good girl."

There it was again. Max's unthinking arrogance. Was it just being a man that caused it? Whatever the cause, it never failed to rub Libby up the wrong way. "I'm not a child, Max. By the way, you never did say why you had to leave Exham in such a hurry."

"I didn't, because," he drawled, "if I told you..."

"I know, you'd have to shoot me. Just tell me if your other responsibilities have anything to do with the dead cyclists, will you?"

He threw a lingering glance in her direction before he answered. "I hope not. I don't think so, but I want you to be careful, Libby. Please don't go poking your nose in where you shouldn't." He waited a beat. "I know you can't resist a mystery, but at least let me know what you're up to."

Max said no more and Libby fell into a kind of hypnotic daze. Half-formed thoughts chased through her head. She'd love to unpack the mystery of Max. He was handsome, wealthy, and long divorced, but showed very little interest in local women. Or men, for that matter. Maybe there was a secret mistress somewhere else. Libby could imagine Max with someone exotic, all long legs and tanned skin, from South America.

Displeased with the idea, she turned her attention to their short relationship. For a while, she'd thought they were getting close, but long walks and longer evenings, with a meal and a bottle of wine or two, had ended in no more than a chaste peck on the cheek. Was that part of the reason Libby found Max so unsettling? Because he didn't want to take things further? Although, of course, she didn't either.

Maybe she should start something with Simon Logan. He seemed flatteringly keen. Would Max be jealous? Libby couldn't decide. His eyes were fixed on the road, his jaw clenched. Libby's eyelids grew heavy. She didn't want any complications. She drifted into sleep.

CHAPTER THREE

Foxgloves

At the hospital, a serious young doctor with floppy hair and horn-rimmed spectacles and a tie tucked between two shirt buttons examined Libby, declared her out of any danger and decreed she could go home. "The hospital's full to bursting, today, after the poisoning. No beds free at all." He yawned. "We think we've pinpointed the poison, though. Digitoxin. It's a compound made from digitalis."

"I'm sorry? What's digitalis? Or the other thing?"

The doctor nodded, brow furrowed in a scholarly expression, transparently gratified to have the chance to explain his newly acquired, expert knowledge. "Digitalis is found in the common foxglove, *Digitalis Purpurea*. That's the Latin name. You can find them easily in woodland."

"Or in people's gardens?"

"Exactly. You'd be surprised how many everyday plants have serious toxic effects. Foxgloves can be both poisonous and beneficial, especially the leaves. Digitalis affects the heart rate."

He thrust his hands into the pockets of crumpled trousers. He looked hardly older than Robert, Libby's son. Did doctors not wear white coats anymore? "Digitoxin must have turned up in the sandwiches or cakes. I believe you only had a small bite, Mrs Forest."

"From an Eccles cake." Libby shivered. She'd never eat one again.

A bleep interrupted. The doctor pulled a small device from his pocket. "Sorry, have to go. Just take it easy for a few days and you'll be fine. Your heart's steady enough."

Max took Libby's arm and walked her to the car. "I suppose you realise what this means for the bakery?"

She closed her eyes. "I've been trying not to think about it, but it's going to be the first place the police look. How could foxglove leaves get into the cyclists' food? Was it deliberate, d'you suppose, or a terrible mistake? Oh dear, I can't seem to think straight."

"Leave it for now. Get a good night's sleep. Things might seem clearer in the morning." Max drove her home.

Mandy was in the kitchen, eyes on stalks, bursting to gossip, but Max cut her short and steered Libby upstairs. "Do you need help getting to bed?"

"I can manage."

"Oh." He leaned forward and kissed her on the cheek. "Sleep well."

***

It was the hammering that woke her. Surfacing from a dreamless sleep, Libby groaned and rolled over. Early light filtered through the curtains. The noise started up again, thudding in her head. Someone was banging on the bedroom door. "What is it?"

Mandy's head appeared. "Sorry to wake you, but your daughter's here."

"Ali?" Libby sat up. That was a mistake. Her head thudded harder. She grabbed the water glass by the bedside table and sipped. Empty. She must have drunk it in the night. With care, she slid one foot out of bed, feeling for the floor. Her stomach lurched.

"Here's the bucket." Mandy was by her side. "Max said this might happen. He said you're to stay in bed. I wasn't going to wake you, but Ali..."

Ali was away at Uni, wasn't she? It couldn't be the holidays already.

"Hi, Mum." Her daughter's head popped round the door. "Your friend, Max, rang. He said you'd been poisoned."

Libby lay back against a pile of pillows. "It's not serious. He shouldn't have worried you."

Ali, eyes wide, hair tousled, grinned. "Of course he should. I've come to look after you. By the way, who was that girl? Why is she dressed like that, with all those studs?"

Guilt crept over Libby. She'd meant to tell Ali about the lodger sleeping in her old bedroom. Somehow, the time had never seemed right. "Mandy works at the bakery with me. She's staying here for a while."

"And when were you thinking of telling me?" Ali raised an eyebrow and leaned over to plump her mother's pillows.

Libby pushed her hand away. "We haven't spoken recently."

Ali's eyes avoided her mother. That last phone call had been heated. She heaved a familiar, exaggerated sigh. "OK, I know I should have rung at the weekend. I was busy."

"With John?" Libby tried to sound non-committal, but the words arrived laced with disapproval. She winced as Ali's eyes narrowed. It was so easy to say the wrong thing.

"Busy, actually. John's been away in Dubai, if you want to know."

"Oh." Libby said no more. Was she being unreasonable? John was a wealthy, sophisticated man more than twenty years older than her daughter. Ali met him when he lectured at the University. He was an expert in philanthropy, apparently, which seemed to be an excuse for the rich to get even richer without feeling guilty.

"Look, Mum, I can see you're feeling lousy. We won't argue just now." Ali bustled about the room, straightening curtains, smoothing the duvet, dusting a mirror with a tissue.

Libby closed her eyes. "I think I'd like to go back to sleep."

"Dry toast. That's what you need."

"Lovely." Anything for a moment's peace. Drowsy, Libby twitched awake as the bedroom door clinked shut. She sighed, closed her eyes and drifted away.

***

Hunger kicked in and she woke. A tray on the bedside table held a slice of cold toast. Libby took a bite. Delicious. Just what she needed, after all. Ali was right.

Libby looked at the clock and threw back the covers. What was happening at the bakery? She reached for her dressing gown and stopped, eyes fixed on the hugely expensive silk pyjamas she wore. She'd bought them a few Christmases ago, as revenge when Trevor gave her a wok. Had Mandy undressed her? *Oh no. Not Max, surely?*

She winced, struggling to remember, and then tugged open a drawer, shuddered at the jumble of clothes inside, and slammed it shut. Max had seen this muddle? And undressed her while she was asleep? She'd never look him in the face again.

Tying the dressing gown tightly, Libby set off downstairs. "Watch out!" The marmalade cat, who offered daily evidence of despising Libby, shot out of the living room and up the stairs, disappearing into the airing cupboard. "That was deliberate, Fuzzy."

A vacuum cleaner hummed as she approached the living room. Ali had wasted no time in getting to grips with the cleaning. Resisting the temptation to tiptoe past into the kitchen, Libby opened the door and planted a kiss on the back of her daughter's head. "Thank you for coming home." She took a breath. "Does your brother know about the—er—the accident?"

"I rang him. He's going to phone you later." Ali switched off the machine and wound the cable neatly. "I hear you poisoned everyone in Exham with your baking yesterday."

"Not me. At least, I hope not."

"Of course it wasn't your fault. I was joking."

"Not very funny, actually. Two people died."

"How awful." Ali's eyes were huge. "Did you know them?"

"Not really. Don't be a ghoul. I don't want to talk about it."

Her daughter pouted. "Very well. Did you know your vacuum cleaner needs bags? I'll pick some up this afternoon. Now, what do you want for lunch? I can stay for a day or so to look after you."

"That's kind of you, but I'm going to work." Libby sniffed the air, scenting coffee.

Mandy arrived, holding the door open with one foot, balancing three mugs on a tray. "You'd better have this before we go to the bakery. I've got a bad feeling about this morning."

CHAPTER FOUR

Cocoa beans

The small yard behind the bakery heaved with police. Libby recognised a middle-aged, overweight constable, all pudding face and small eyes, as one of Joe's team. He held up a hand the size of a dinner plate. "You can't come in, Ma'am, I'm afraid."

Frank handed keys to a tall woman in white overalls. He looked terrible, with red-rimmed eyes, his brow furrowed. Mournful, he shook his head at Libby. "They're going to search the bakery." He'd aged overnight. He'd become an old man, and his voice quivered. "This will put us out of business." His lip was trembling. "I'm sorry, Libby. Just when you were about to get started."

It was true, then. The police were blaming the bakery for Kevin Batty's death. Frank's business, built up over dozens of years, had hit the dust, and both Libby and Mandy were out of a job. A shock of reality punched Libby in the chest. A closed bakery meant the end of the chocolate project. Her wonderful new career had died before it even came to life. Mandy's eyes, lined with black kohl, were enormous in her white face. "What will we do?"

The constable—Ian Smith was his name, Libby remembered—looked vaguely sympathetic. Frank was well known and popular in the town. "We need to ask you some questions at the police station, sir."

Frank's body slumped. Libby forced a cheerful smile as she patted his arm. "Don't worry, we'll find out what happened."

Constable Smith's concern failed to extend to Libby. "Don't go interfering, ma'am. We'll be talking to all of you, and you'll be better off waiting quietly at home until then."

"Last time..." Libby bit off her words. Reminding the officer how badly the police had failed before would just antagonise him. "Are you suggesting we're all suspects?"

"We can't discuss it yet. We'll talk to you later today. Now, let me have your phone number and go on home."

Mandy's mouth hung open as the police hustled the baker away. "They can't think it was Frank?"

"It looks like it. Come on, let's go. We need to find out what really happened."

***

Libby's year in Exham had taught her who was likely to know most about the area. In a moment of genius, she lured Ali out of the house, sending her to Bath in search of new curtains for the living room, picked up the phone, and issued an invitation to Marina.

While she waited, Libby started on her new, hastily formed plan. The moment of despair at the bakery had soon passed. She had no idea how she was going to sell her wares, but she wasn't about to give in and abandon the chocolate dream at the first obstacle. She was going to make up a new batch and find an outlet somehow, even if she had to hawk her wares all over England.

Mandy wandered aimlessly round the house, switching on televisions and turning them off again. Libby tracked her down in the bathroom and grabbed an arm, just in time to stop her painting each nail a different shade of mauve. "Mandy, come and help me in the kitchen. I'll need an assistant if I'm going to make this project work."

"Not giving up, then, Mrs F?"

"You bet I'm not. Did you see how those free samples disappeared? There's a real market for original chocolates. We're going to make them, even if we can't sell them at Frank's. Maybe some of the shops in Bath will stock them, instead." Libby set up the chocolate grinder and tipped warm beans inside.

As they worked, the hours raced past, meals forgotten, until Marina arrived. She wafted in on a cloud of Youth Dew, resplendent in a purple kimono, amber beads jangling on her spectacular chest. "Darling Libby, you look ghastly," she gushed. "We were all so worried."

"Actually, I'm perfectly all right, now, thank you."

"Well, if there's anything you need, you only have to ask. Though I've only got a few minutes. I'm getting my hair done." Marina settled herself more comfortably on the sofa and got down to business. "Now, do tell me everything. I heard it wasn't food poisoning, but real poison. How extraordinary. Just imagine!"

Marina wore the permanent air of unconscious, effortless superiority of someone who'd spent her life nurtured and cherished, never denied any pleasure she desired. As a result, good-humoured, extravert, and a pillar of Exham society, she provided a never-ending source of the very best gossip. Libby forgave Marina's sloth, although one day, she'd pluck up the courage to tell her friend to take her own dog for walks. Poor Shipley would never get beyond the garden gate, if Libby didn't take him.

Marina sipped at a glass of sherry. "Who would have thought it of Frank?"

"Don't be ridiculous. Frank wouldn't kill anyone." Kind, monosyllabic Frank could hardly bring himself to squash a wasp.

Marina helped herself to a cup cake. "Who else could it be? One minute, everyone's buzzing along the road like a swarm of starving bees in Lycra, and the next, they eat Frank's food and half the cycling club ends up in hospital. Everyone knows Frank quarrelled with Kevin Batty, years ago. He must have decided to get his own back."

A chill crept up Libby's neck. If Frank had a motive, he was in big trouble. "What did they fall out about?"

"Well." Marina sat forward, settling the heavy orange beads more comfortably, face animated. "Kevin was a very rich man. One of the big farmers in the area. Plenty of land, darling, all in the family. Of course, he didn't farm it himself. He rented most of it out."

Libby blinked. "You're kidding." She'd only met Kevin a few times, but anyone who looked less like a wealthy landowner would be hard to find. Everything the man wore seemed to be made for someone ten pounds heavier, as though he bought every item of clothes second hand.

Marina's laugh tinkled. "You'd know if you'd grown up around here. The Battys own half the county, and my husband handles their affairs.

Kevin's finger was in plenty of pies; sheep farms, dairy, and just a few acres of wheat."

Libby topped up Marina's glass. "Come to think of it, I've seen Batty lorries on the motorway."

"That's right." Marina wrinkled her nose. "Not the cleanest on the road, I'm afraid. Now," she swept on, "where was I? Oh, yes, Kevin used to supply flour to the bakery, years ago. Then, he had the falling out with Frank. It started with darts, in the pub. Kevin accused Frank of using weighted darts. Or was it Frank accusing Kevin? Can't quite remember. Anyway," Marina shrugged, dismissive of such details. "They had a fight. They were both drunk, and Frank gave Kevin a bloody nose. The next thing Frank knew, Kevin hiked the price of his flour sky-high and nearly bankrupted the bakery."

Mandy called from the kitchen. "The grinder's finished."

Chocolate scented the air as Libby opened the huge metal grinder and scooped out the paste. Marina rustled, close behind. "Oh, I didn't know you made your chocolates from actual cocoa beans. Can I taste?"

"Not yet, I'm afraid. It's too bitter at this stage. Inedible." Libby let heavy blobs fall onto a vast marble board.

Marina glanced at her expensive watch. "Look at the time. I'm going to be late." She gathered up scarves and bags. "Now, don't worry, I'll let myself out." She was gone, slightly unsteady, leaving a heavy trail of perfume.

Libby swooped on the heap of chocolate paste, scraping and turning it with vigour, watching for the shine that would tell her it was ready for use. "I'm afraid everyone in town knows food poisoning killed the cyclists," she told Mandy. "The bakery's getting the blame."

Mandy's eyes were huge. "I don't know what I'll do for money, without that job."

"Well, I'm sure it won't be for long. Everyone knows Frank's fanatical about hygiene."

Mandy was biting her thumbnail. "It's not just Frank. We're all under suspicion. No one's going to want our chocolates, now."

CHAPTER FIVE

Pizza and salad

Ali arrived back from Bath early. "I found just what you need in the first shop." In minutes, she was bent over the ancient, hardly-used sewing machine, shortening curtains.

Too restless to stay indoors, Libby made an excuse. "I need Marmite to settle my stomach," she announced, and drove to the supermarket. The place was overheated and crowded. Libby leaned on the trolley, wishing she'd stayed at home.

"What are you doing here? You should be taking it easy."

Libby jumped. "Max! How do you manage to keep creeping up on me like that?"

"You were miles away. By the way, did you mean to put five boxes of cornflakes in your trolley."

How did that happen? "I'm hiding from my daughter's ministrations." That was unkind. "Oh dear, I didn't mean that the way it sounded. It's just that Ali's so organised. Unlike me. She arrived yesterday and she hasn't stopped cleaning yet. She's hanging curtains as we speak."

Max replaced cornflake packets on the shelf. "Heaven help anyone who tries to organise you, Libby Forest."

"What's that supposed to mean?"

"No need to get on your high horse. I mean you're a very capable woman who knows what she wants. By the way, how's the stomach?"

"Better. I suppose I should thank you for putting me to bed." Now, she sounded ungracious. "Sorry. I really am grateful." Libby couldn't forget the silk pyjamas, but if she didn't mention them, maybe Max wouldn't, either.

"If you want to get away from your daughter for a bit, come over to my place. There's pizza in the freezer."

"Pizza? Really?"

"Forget your culinary standards for once and come down to my level."

"I could cook."

He raised an eyebrow. "If you like. You choose."

Why was she making work? The habit of a lifetime. Crazy. Time to stop trying to please everyone. "Pizza sounds wonderful."

He grinned. "That wasn't so hard, was it? You don't have to be perfect all the time, you know."

Libby concentrated on the pizza on her plate. She'd made a salad, squeezing lemon into olive oil, adding a touch of honey and mustard, and a pinch of salt, grateful Max hadn't refused to eat the food she made. At least he didn't think she was a poisoner. "You're looking better," Max said. "Nothing like junk food to settle the digestion."

"How's Joe?"

"They're letting him out in a couple of days, and I said I'd go and visit. We're almost on speaking terms at the moment, so long as we don't mention anything about his work or mine, especially the local thugs he's been watching."

Libby shivered. "I've got an interview with one of Joe's colleagues, soon. Ian Smith. About the Eccles cake."

"Are you interviewing the police, or they, you?"

"Very funny. Apparently, I'm a suspect."

"OK to talk about it?"

"With the police, or with you?"

"Either. Both."

"There's not much I can say. It's all a complete mystery to me. I mean, poisoning a whole cycle club. Who'd do that? It's ridiculous to suggest Frank would. It'll ruin his business."

Max took the plates out, calling back, "You're sure it's deliberate, then?"

Libby followed, a wine glass in each hand. "Well, I can't believe the food was contaminated by mistake. We're always so careful. We know it's not the sandwiches, but that doesn't stop people blaming the bakery. We could be shut down for good."

"How do you know it's not the sandwiches?"

Enraged, Libby glared. "Of course it wasn't."

"No. You don't want it to be. Come on Libby, put that logical mind of yours to work. Digitalis, or digitoxin, or whatever that doctor called it. How would you get hold of it?"

Libby thought hard. "He said it was used as medicine, so presumably you could get it from your GP. There's always the chemist, but you'd need a prescription."

Max chimed in. "Or the internet. Could you make it yourself?"

"Did they teach you much about poisons in secret service school?"

"Sadly, no, not unless you count polonium."

"I think we're looking at something easier to get your hands on than radio-active isotopes."

Max stacked plates in the dishwasher. "It sounds as though we're investigating again. Ramshore and Forest, private investigations a speciality. No stone unturned. We should join forces and start a business. You'll need a second string if the bakery has to close."

Libby put her head on one side. "Forest and Ramshore sounds better. Anyway, we can't just leave it to the police. Manpower's always short, and unless they're convinced it's nothing to do with the shop, I don't think they'll look too hard elsewhere."

"Forest and Ramshore it is, then. Where shall we start? With the poison?"

"It's as good a place as any, though there are a couple of other things we ought to think about."

"Like, what do Kevin and Vince have in common that made them targets? Why were they both killed?"

"Exactly. And what about Joe and the rest of the club? It could have been a random attack, maybe trying to frighten them, that went too far." It was a mess. "How could the poisoner even be sure anyone would die? This is going to take a while. I'd better warn my daughter."

She rang Ali's mobile. "I'm going to be late. Max and I are going over ideas for the chocolate business."

"Yeah, Mum." That was definitely a snigger. "Are you coming home tonight?"

"Of course." Libby's face burned.

"Mandy and I are fine. She's been filling me in on a few things." That sounded ominous. "Oh, and Fuzzy's sitting on my lap."

"That cat never sits with me. She hates me. She tried to trip me on the stairs again."

"See you later, Mum." Ali was laughing as she broke the connection.

Max didn't bother to pretend he hadn't heard. "I take it you have permission to stay out late?"

Libby dropped her phone in a pocket. "Fire up that laptop. We've got poisons to trace."

***

Poison-hunting on the internet revealed few new facts. Digitoxin could be easily extracted from the crushed leaves of foxgloves, and was found in some prescribed medication for heart disease. Several cups of coffee later, with little more to show for their efforts than a list of medications containing digitalis extract under a confusing number of names, Libby sighed and stretched. "We're not really very much farther forward. We need a better plan."

Max flipped the lid on the laptop. "Suggestions?"

"Well, the poison's just the method. What about a reason for killing Kevin and Vince? I suppose you weren't at school with half the cycling club?"

"Afraid not. Most of them moved here in the last twenty years or so. Your friend Marina's husband's a member, though."

Marina hadn't mentioned that. Presumably, Henry had been at work, not cycling through the lanes that day. Max cleared his throat. "There's something I was going to tell you before, on the beach, when my phone rang."

"Yes?"

He wouldn't meet her eyes. "I've got to go away again, tomorrow. Just for a day or two."

"Oh?" What did he expect her to say?

"Well, there's Bear."

"Not leaving him with your farmer friend, this time?"

"Can't keep abusing the hospitality. For one thing, the animal eats like a rugby player."

Libby wasn't going to make it easy for him. "So, what are you suggesting?"

"Bear's used to you. I wondered if you'd come over to keep an eye on him. He lives outside in the shed unless it's freezing cold. That double layer of fur keeps him warm, but he needs company and plenty of exercise, and he likes you."

Libby laughed. Bear was fast asleep, his massive head trapping her feet, as if he'd already claimed her. "Let him stay with me for a while. We managed before, and I'll take him for a long run every day."

"What about your carpets?"

"I'll get them replaced and send you a bill."

"It's a deal."

Max thumped the dog gently on the shoulder. "See, Bear, I told you she'd take you in. Be a good guest. No chewing the furniture."

"How long will you be gone?"

"Can't be sure, I'm afraid. As a sweetener, would you like to borrow the Land Rover? Better than letting Bear climb all over your car."

"You won't need it?"

"It's quicker by train." Heading out of the country, then. Libby knew better than to ask where he was going. She was pleased they were back on some sort of steady footing. Good friends, nothing more. Wasn't that just what she wanted? "Thanks. My car's desperate for a service. I'll get Alan at the garage to pick it up tomorrow."

CHAPTER SIX

Breakfast

Mandy and Ali gossiped in the kitchen next morning, brewing coffee, eating breakfast cereal and giggling. "Morning, Mum. Did you have a good evening?" Cue more giggling.

"Hangover, Mrs F?" Libby heaved a heavy sigh, feeling like a visitor in her own house. She'd rise above it. She kissed Ali on the cheek, smiled at Mandy, grabbed a mug of coffee, scooped up Fuzzy and retired to the sitting room. Bear padded behind, tail wagging.

The house had seemed quiet when Libby first arrived a year ago, but then Mandy moved in as a lodger and brought it back to life. Now, with Ali home and Bear visiting, the tiny cottage seemed full to overflowing.

Ali joined her mother on the sofa. Fuzzy jumped down from Libby's arms to rub herself against Ali, purring, orange tail flicking in the air. Bear, making himself at home, stretched out across the floor, filling the room from door to window. Libby watched her daughter stroke the side of Fuzzy's face and wondered how she'd ever managed to produce a child so unlike herself. Where did that ash blonde hair come from? It was cut short and spiky, emphasising Ali's round cheeks and full lips. Her daughter had turned into a beauty. "What's wrong, Ali?"

Instead of answering, Ali wrinkled her nose and pouted. Libby recognised the expression. It had first appeared when Ali, aged three, struggled with an early drawing of a house. It came back whenever she was anxious or faced with a difficult challenge. "Was there another reason you came home? Apart from the need to look after your sick mother?"

Ali looked guilty. Libby had hit the nail on the head. "I was worried about you, Mum, truly. Dad always said you can't look after yourself."

"Well, that's what he thought." Libby shrugged. No need to dump her feelings about Trevor on their daughter. She kept talking, giving Ali a chance to collect her thoughts. "Anyway, I'm glad you get on well with Mandy, though she'll be moving out soon, I expect. She's only staying here until she can afford a flat of her own."

Ali's eyes were suspiciously shiny. Libby stepped over Bear and dropped on to the sofa, one arm round her daughter. For once, Ali didn't shrug it off or move away. "Tell me what's going on. Is it boyfriend problems?" That older man. She'd known he'd break Ali's heart. "Is it John?"

Ali managed a watery laugh. "No, Mum. We broke up ages ago. I told you." She hadn't, but Libby let it go. Ali grabbed Fuzzy and buried her face in the cat's fur. "John wasn't really that interested in philanthropy. At least, not for himself. He just liked to give lectures about it. Well paid lectures."

"Good job you saw through him, then. But, if he's not the problem, what's wrong?"

"I don't think I'm doing the right thing."

"You mean, at Uni? Is it the course?"

Ali blushed. "History's all very well, but I want to make some sort of a difference. How's history going to help when children are starving on the other side of the world?" She looked up, straight into Libby's face, her own cheeks glowing. "I want to do something really useful."

Libby chose her words with care. "I think that would be very worthwhile. You could get a job in the voluntary sector when you finish your degree."

Ali rolled her eyes. "I knew you'd say that. Just because you always did what people told you." Her words struck home. She was right. Libby had always expected good behaviour to lead to happiness. What a shame she'd believed it for so long.

Ali spoke slowly, as though Libby was very old or deaf. "I'm nothing like you. I want to do things that matter, while I'm still young enough. Not live a boring life, like you and Dad, and then die. I won't waste any more time doing something I don't care about."

Was that truly how Libby's life seemed to Ali? Boring and useless? Libby counted to ten and kept her voice level. "Why don't you carry on at Uni to the end of the year, then see what you want to do?"

Before the words left her mouth, she knew it was the wrong thing to say. Ali's face flamed. She pushed her mother's arm away. "You don't understand. You never have. Anyway, it's too late. I've already left Uni."

Libby stared. "Left? Officially?"

"That's right." Ali was defiant, eyes blazing. "I can't go back, even if I wanted to. And I've got a job."

"A what?"

"That's right, a job. I'm going to help build schools in the rain forest. I've come home to pack and then Andy's coming to pick me up."

"You mean, you're leaving the country? And who's Andy?" Libby was struggling to take it in.

"Just a friend. Why shouldn't I go? I'm not a child anymore."

Before Libby could gather her arguments, Ali dumped the cat on the floor, flounced out of the room and stamped upstairs.

***

Libby needed time to think. "What am I supposed to say, Bear?" The dog whined and nuzzled her legs. "She's just throwing away her life."

Libby would never have defied her own parents. Things were different, in those days. She'd gone to University, taken a degree in social science, met Trevor and slipped into a quiet domestic life. She'd never even used that degree. Maybe Ali had a point.

Bear was pacing round the room. Fuzzy had disappeared, probably sulking in the airing cupboard. Libby longed to talk to someone. She needed advice, but there was no one around to help. Libby shooed Bear out into the garden, following behind, hoping fresh air would bring inspiration. She snatched weeds from the border, tossing them on the compost heap.

The breeze blew hair into her eyes and she pushed it away, irritated. Of course she didn't want Ali to turn into a doormat. Libby kicked a stone. She'd wasted a lot of her life. The only things she didn't regret were her children. Bringing up Robert and Ali to healthy adulthood, with strong minds of

43

their own, were achievements she'd always think of with pride.

She needed to make peace with her daughter. She wiped her hands on her jeans and went back indoors, to tap on Ali's bedroom door. Ali, red-eyed, blocked her way.

"Maybe I'd better help you pack."

Ali stared, frowning. "Seriously?" Libby nodded. "You're not going to try and stop me?"

"Ali, I don't want you to spend your life trying to please other people. If you're determined to do this, and you're doing it for you and not for this Andy, I'll give you my blessing." *And worry about you every moment you're away.*

Ali wiped her nose on her sleeve. "Good." She muttered. "I thought you were going to cause a fuss."

An hour later, Ali sat on her rucksack while Libby eased the zip round the lumps and bumps of t-shirts, earphones, boots and the other essentials of life in the wild. It turned out Ali had been planning this for weeks, if not months, ever since she met Andy. "He's very quiet. Thoughtful, you know, Mum. He's from Canada, and he got me the job." She showed Libby the paperwork. Tickets, letters of introduction, a signed contract.

Libby couldn't find anything wrong. "I just wish you'd told me sooner."

"You'd have tried to stop me."

"Will I see him?"

"Soon. He's coming here and then we're catching the train at midday."

The doorbell rang. Ali gave Libby a brief kiss on the cheek, hoisted up the huge rucksack, waved to a stunned Mandy, and disappeared.

Libby climbed the stairs, head reeling, back to the room her daughter had slept in. It had all happened so fast, she couldn't take it in. Slowly, painfully, she tidied away the few remaining bits and pieces they'd failed to stuff into the rucksack. A lump of iron seemed to have stuck in her chest, making it hard to breathe. When was she going to see her daughter again?

She blew her nose, determined not to cry. All that cleaning, the fussing over curtains, had all been Ali's way of saying goodbye. If only Libby had understood. She stretched, relieving the ache in her back, and something caught her eye. *What's that?* A drawer in Ali's bedside table was stuck, half open. One corner of a brown envelope, peeking out at an angle, stopped it sliding shut.

Libby pulled the drawer open and pulled at the envelope, turning it over, registering Ali's name on the front. It was unsealed, the contents still inside.

CHAPTER SEVEN

Mutton

Libby recognised that writing. She held the brown envelope in one hand, eyes on Trevor's familiar neat, precise pen strokes, unsure. She should leave it alone. It wasn't addressed to her. Everyone knew no good came of checking your children's private papers, but how could any mother resist a peek inside a package sent by her dead husband to their daughter?

At least the envelope wasn't sealed, so Libby didn't have to steam it open. With one guilty glance back at the bedroom door, she tipped it up and let the contents slide onto the bed.

Just two sheets of paper fell out. One was a handwritten letter, the other, an estate agent's advertisement for a house. A house in Leeds. Libby stared. The house was nothing special; just the kind of lofty Victorian building often divided into flats for students. But in Leeds? The family had no connections there.

Libby dropped the advertisement and picked up the letter, curiously reluctant to read anything written by her husband. It was short and dated two years ago. *Dear Alison,* it began. He always used his daughter's full name. *Before you go off to Uni, I want you to have this, in case you ever need it. The house is in your name. Robert owns another, just like it. You must keep the house for five years. You can sell it then, if you like, but please use the agent mentioned on the enclosed document.*

This is between you and me. Your mother will have my estate should I die, which I have no intention of doing at present, but this is for you alone.

You may need a bolt-hole one day.

With love,

Dad.

Libby pored over the letter, but subsequent readings made no more sense than the first. There was no reason why Trevor shouldn't buy a house and put it in Ali's name. Perhaps it was a thoughtful thing to do, making sure his daughter had a foot on the housing ladder. But why bother to keep it a secret? And why buy a house so far away, in Leeds? They'd lived in London all their married life.

Libby shook her head, perplexed by yet another shock from the grave. Who would have thought it of rigid, respectable Trevor? Six months ago, she'd discovered he'd emptied his bank accounts and left nothing but debts. It meant Libby couldn't

47

redecorate the ghastly bathroom, but she'd survived. Now, this? What else had Trevor hidden from his wife?

Libby sat on the bed, legs crossed, thinking. Trevor was a control freak. He'd kept her under his thumb, refusing to discuss work, or anything else for that matter. As a result, she had little idea what his job entailed, except that he was an insurance agent. How had he managed to acquire a couple of houses his wife knew nothing about?

It seemed strange, finding the letter sticking out of a drawer. Why had Ali left it behind? She hadn't really tried to hide it. Maybe she'd wanted her mother to know, but wouldn't directly disobey her father. Libby made a thumbs-up sign. *Good solution, Ali.*

She folded the two sheets of paper, replaced them in the envelope and took the package to her room, sliding it into her handbag. She straightened. Were there any more surprises from Trevor? She still had a few of his things. Maybe she should look through them.

She opened the door to the third bedroom she used as a study, where she kept some of Trevor's old clothes. Full of shocked guilt at her husband's sudden death, she'd left them in the wardrobe in the London house, to deal with later. When she came to Exham, the removal firm had bundled them up and hung them straight in the wardrobe. She hadn't touched them since. Maybe there were more clues to the Trevor she'd never known among his old clothes.

She caught her breath, smelling the faintest trace of Old Spice clinging to an ancient corduroy jacket. Trevor had worn that old brown favourite every weekend, refusing to let Libby throw it out even when it grew old and shabby. She'd bought a new one, identical, once, as a birthday surprise. Trevor told her to take it back to the shop.

Pictures flashed behind Libby's eyes. She remembered Trevor one Sunday, complaining the roast potatoes were cold, retiring to his study, and shoving papers swiftly into his briefcase as she brought his coffee. The image lingered. He'd looked annoyed, his cheeks unusually flushed. Did the papers belong to his insurance clients, as she'd always supposed, or were they something less innocent?

Libby tossed the jacket on a chair. It was going out, along with anything else that reminded her of her husband. She grabbed one item after another, shaking them, feeling in the pockets for any stray clues to a secret life.

When the solicitor had told Libby she was broke, she hadn't thought to investigate. She'd just accepted that Trevor had indulged himself, while at the same time complaining about every penny Libby spent on anything he called a selfish luxury, like new clothes. Now, she had to know more.

Slowly, a pile of old receipts and train tickets grew on the desk. She'd found nothing unexpected, so far.

Wait! What was that? She smoothed out a crumpled slip of paper, a receipt from a hire car company in Leeds. Evidence of that secret life Trevor had lived?

Libby's head buzzed with questions. Why had her husband bought houses in Leeds, when they lived in London? Who lived in the house he'd passed on to Ali and why had he told Ali not to put the house up for sale for five years?

Maybe he was having an affair. Did he have a mistress, living up in Leeds? He would want her to keep the house for a few years after his death, for security. The thought made Libby burn with fury. He hadn't cared much about his wife's security.

She bundled the pile of clothes into a charity plastic bag and dumped them beside the front door. A plan was forming in her head. She had clues, now. All she had to was follow them to find out what Trevor was up to. She'd give it a few days until she had her car back, all serviced and ready for a trip to Leeds. Then, she'd make the trip and surprise whoever lived in the house.

CHAPTER EIGHT

Mushroom omelettes

Looking after Bear gave Libby the excuse she needed to wander along the seafront, doing nothing in particular. She'd pick up the car later, ready for the trip to Leeds. The Exham promenade bustled with early seaside visitors. Too early in the year for families with children, who were still in school, the pavement filled with older people, more interested in the coffee shops in the High Street than the stalls that teemed with plastic spades and Union flags.

Libby strolled in the sunshine, Bear at her side, head so full of mixed speculation about Trevor, Ali and the cycling club that at first she didn't hear the voice calling her name. "Libby. Over here." Angela Miles, grey hair piled on top of her head, wire-rimmed glasses dangling on a string round her neck, poked her head out of the door of the seafront cafe.

Libby liked Angela, who never asked for favours or bullied people. "Sorry. Thinking about something."

"I see Max Ramshore's gone away again, and left you with his dog."

"I'm just looking after Bear for a few days. I like his company."

"Mandy's still staying with you too. I don't know where you get your energy." Angela ducked as a seagull swooped past, on the look-out for easy food. She sounded odd, off balance.

Libby examined her friend's face. The eyes looked brighter than usual. "Is there something wrong?"

"Not at all." Angela beamed. "In fact, I'm doing something I should have done years ago. The trouble is, it's making me nervous."

"Sounds exciting." Libby steered her friend towards the tables set out at the entrance to the pier. "We need coffee while you tell me all about it."

"I've just had some."

"There's always room for another cup. Or," scanning the list on the blackboard, "even better, hot chocolate."

Settled at a corner table, a steaming cup stacked with calories in front of her, Libby could wait no longer. "Now then, out with it. What's up?"

"It's all your fault, you know."

Libby blinked. "Me? Why? Have I offended you?"

"No, of course not. Quite the opposite. I've been watching you, since you came to Exham. You dash about, doing what you want, whether other people approve or not. Your book's been published and you're a proper author, now. You solve mysteries, and you're starting up in business." Angela stirred her chocolate. "Watching you made me realise I don't have to slow down, just because I'm not thirty any more. I'm going to do something with my life."

She finished her drink and set the mug down on its saucer. "Did you know my husband, Geoff, was a composer?"

Libby racked her brains. Geoffrey Miles. The name rang a bell. "Not the Geoffrey Miles who wrote music for that film that picked up all the Oscars? What was it called?"

"An Honourable Gentleman." Angela trailed one finger in a splash of milk on the table. "I need to explain. I was very young when I married Geoff. He swept me off my feet with his genius. He was a lecturer at the University, and I could see he would make his name in the music world, while I was just a student."

She drew a shape in the spilled milk. Libby thought it was a treble clef. "My music always came second, of course, because he was a rising star and I was just competent. His friends, fellow lecturers, were all brilliant, but he stood out."

Angela used a paper napkin to mop up the drops of milk. "You see, unlike me, you've been brave enough to start again on your own." She turned bright green eyes on Libby. "You've shaken up Exham, that's for sure."

Libby drained the last drop of cream from her mug and wiped froth off her lips. "And upset a few people."

Angela piled their cups on a tray. "I've decided to be more like you. I'm not going to waste any more time. I'm starting a series of concerts."

Libby shooed away a couple of hopeful pigeons. "If you've got time, let me cook you lunch, and you can tell me more. Mandy's out and my daughter's flying visit is over."

Angela beamed. "That would be wonderful."

***

Libby tossed a salad, flipped mushroom omelettes and poured chilled white wine into two large glasses. Angela rootled in her giant tote handbag and pulled out a thick file. "I wanted to show you this. Geoff died ten years ago, but I only found this the other day when I was up in the loft. I've been carrying it around, wondering what to do. Now, I know."

She laid the papers on the table. Libby leaned forward. "Manuscript paper?"

"Some of Geoff's music. I had a call from his old agent the other day. First time I'd heard from him for years. He wants to do a memorial concert, ten years after Geoff died, using Geoff's old friends. I said no, of course. I'd have to persuade people to join in, organise rehearsals, help with the arrangements for the concert. It all seemed too much bother."

She grinned. "I changed my mind. I used to manage Geoff, when we were younger. I dealt with his travel, venues, schedules, everything. Why shouldn't I do it now? I've decided to put on concerts and use them to raise money for charity."

Angela looked ten years younger. She rustled the manuscript paper. "I thought I'd start with this quintet. It hasn't been played in public often. It was one of the last things Geoff wrote. We were about to perform it on the day he ran his car off the road."

"Wow. That's some undertaking."

"I've already got the performers to agree. Geoff's sister's coming, she's a violinist, I still play the violin a bit, and Geoff's nephew will play clarinet. Geoff would have liked that. It's all on track."

"When's the concert?"

"In a few weeks. Do you think I'm doing the right thing?" Angela frowned, suddenly anxious.

"Of course you are. It's a wonderful idea." Libby flicked through the papers on the table, one finger following the lines of notes, wishing she could read music and hear the melody in her head.

She tried to figure out the directions scribbled above the lines. *Allegretto. Diminuendo.* "I wish I knew what all these Italian words mean." Her finger stopped moving. "That's funny."

"What do you mean?"

"Look. On the last few pages, the handwriting's different. I can't make things out at all."

Angela balanced the reading glasses on her nose and squinted at the manuscript. "I see what you mean. I hadn't noticed, before. How very odd. Geoff was meticulous. His notation was always neat and tidy."

She flicked from one page to another. "Wait." Her brow cleared. "I remember now. Geoff must have been working on this, when he sprained his wrist, skiing. Look, see how shaky that crotchet is?"

Libby hardly knew a crotchet from a croquet mallet, but even she could see the composer had struggled to write legibly. Angela shuffled the pages into a neat pile. "I never let anyone perform the music again. I thought it had some sort of a curse on it. You know, because Geoff died. I can see now, I was being silly. We're going to have a wonderful concert, and we'll play this piece for Geoff."

CHAPTER NINE

Poached eggs

The mornings seemed very empty, now the bakery was closed. Libby perched on a kitchen stool, breakfast mug in hand, while Mandy rotated marmalade, chocolate spread and peanut butter, munching one slice of toast after another. "It's weird," she said. "It was such a pain, having to wake up at the crack of dawn. I thought I hated it, but now I kind of, like, miss it."

Libby swirled boiling water, added a drop of vinegar and lowered eggs into the pan. "I know what you mean. Sometimes, I had to put the alarm clock on the other side of the room, so I'd have to get out of bed."

She rescued a slice of toast from Mandy's chocolate spread and centred a poached egg on top. "Here, get some protein down you."

Mandy gulped it down. "Mmm. Trouble is, now I don't have to get up, I seem to wake even earlier, and I can't get back to sleep because I'm worrying about getting another job."

Libby ground salt on her egg. "It must be even worse for Frank. I don't think he ever missed a morning at the shop. Did he even go on holiday?"

"Not so far as I know." Mandy licked her fingers. "I suppose his wife will look after him. At least he won't be lonely."

"I've a feeling Frank's happiest in the shop. He likes a bit of peace and quiet."

Mandy laughed and a mouthful of tea went down the wrong way. She mopped streaming eyes. "Are you and Max going to investigate the murders, like last time?"

Libby tapped one finger on the side of her cup. How much should she involve Mandy? She'd hate to drag the girl into any sort of danger, but Mandy had a sharp brain and she'd grown up in Exham. She could be useful.

Mandy interrupted Libby's train of thought. "I know that look. You're already on the trail, and it's not fair to leave me out. Anyway, there's nothing else for me to do all day." She pointed at the kitchen clock. "It's not even nine o'clock, yet. I suppose I'll have to sign on, but what will I do the rest of the time?"

"I'm sure the shop will open again..." Libby sounded unconvincing, even to herself.

Mandy blew a puff of air through her mouth. "No chance. Pritchards will muscle in on the bakery."

Libby wrinkled her brow. She'd heard that name, somewhere. "The chain of grocery shops and bakeries?"

"They're all over the West Country."

"How do you know they're interested in Frank's shop?"

"Per-lease." Mandy tapped her nose. "I have my sources."

"Which are?"

"My friend Steve's got a mate who works at Pritchards. They're buying up all the empty shops, as cheap as possible. He says they'd do anything to get hold of a thriving business like Frank's. It's meant to be secret, but..."

"I now, nothing stays secret for long in Exham."

"See, I can help."

"How does that help, exactly?"

Mandy banged a triumphant hand on the work surface. "What if they're poisoning people deliberately, to get Frank's bakery blamed, so they can buy him out?"

Libby spluttered. "That's crazy, Mandy. They're a perfectly respectable business. They won't kill people just to open a shop."

"Maybe they're backed by the Mafia."

"In Exham? I doubt it, somehow. By the way, who's this Steve? Do I know him?"

"Oh, just someone I know from that club I go to on Fridays." Mandy jumped down and busied herself tidying the kitchen.

"The Goth club? I suppose he listens to that music you like?"

"You mean Katatonia?"

"Er, possibly." If they were responsible for the screeching from Mandy's bedroom. "Anyway, I'd like to hear what he has to say. Your idea's crazy, but maybe we should eliminate it."

"Come to the club."

"You're joking. I'm far too old and I value my hearing. Could we go round and talk to Steve at home instead?"

Mandy beamed, and Libby realised she'd been played. "I'll ring him. I think his mum's away at the moment."

Libby wiped down the kitchen counters. "He lives at home, then?"

"Can't afford a flat, can he? No one can, these days."

"Then, that's what we'll do this evening. But, meanwhile, if you really want to help?"

"Course, I do."

"Make me a list of the people in the cycle club and anything you know about them. Especially Vince and Kevin. I'm wondering why those two died, but no one else."

Mandy narrowed her eyes. "Kevin's lived around here for ever, but Vince is new. Don't know much about him, but maybe I can find out."

Libby folded the cloth and placed it neatly over the edge of the sink. She'd need to make sure Mandy didn't run into danger. "Take it easy. We're looking for a poisoner. A killer. I don't want to have to tell your mother I put you in harm's way. Just write down everything you know."

Mandy nodded, but there was something about the determined angle of her chin that worried Libby. She'd never forgive herself if Mandy ended up into trouble. "I mean it, Mandy. Take care."

"I can look after myself."

There wasn't much more Libby could say. Mandy was stubborn, and a landlady couldn't lock her lodger in the house. She left matters there, and set off in search of Marina. She was certain her friend had more information to give, if only Libby could pin her down long enough to drag it out.

At least she knew where to find her. Marina had recently watched a Panorama programme and decided she needed to get fit. "Don't want to die of high blood pressure or heart disease, darling."

The difficulty seemed to be finding a regime that involved a minimum of exertion. Dismissing dieting, dog-walking and running as undignified and exhausting, Marina turned back to an old passion. She'd learned to ride horses at her expensive boarding school, alongside minor royalty. "At least I can ride sitting down," she announced. "Far more comfortable." Today, she'd be out at the stables, taking a quiet hack around the lanes.

***

The drive took Libby over an hour. Why Marina travelled all the way to a tiny village near Shepton Mallet for her lessons, Libby had no idea, unless it was in the hope of meeting celebrity jockeys riding out on the gallops.

A string of well-fed, mild-mannered horses puffed up a hill. Libby slowed. That had to be Marina bringing up the rear, in a luminous orange jacket. Libby drove round the corner, parked in sight of the stables, and settled down to wait. The open window let the country smells of hay and horse manure fill the car. Libby tried to decide whether she loved or hated them.

The single file of horses clattered into the yard. They were huge—much bigger than Libby expected. She'd never before been within a hundred yards of a horse. She wasn't letting those hooves anywhere near her feet.

Plucking up courage, she left the safety of the Land Rover, hovering out of range as stable hands led the horses into nearby stalls and riders drifted away. Marina remained, her back turned to Libby, deep in conversation. Libby touched her friend's shoulder. "Hello."

Marina swung round, mouth open. "Libby. What the—what are you doing here?" A crimson stain crept up her cheeks.

Her companion was new to Libby. Heavily built, immaculate in full riding kit, his weather-beaten, fleshy face crowned by a shock of snow-white hair, he tapped a riding whip lightly against mud-splashed leather boots. Libby flashed her warmest smile. "Sorry to interrupt. I hoped I'd find you out here."

Marina swallowed, neck tendons working. Her eyes flickered to her companion and back. "Here I am. Taking riding lessons."

"It looks like fun."

The stranger turned full beam on Libby. "I don't believe we've met." His voice rumbled deep in his chest. "My name's Wendlebury. Chesterton Wendlebury."

CHAPTER TEN

Pasta and spotted dick

Chesterton Wendlebury secured the best table in the Monmouth Arms, near the wood fire, explained he had urgent business and left. Marina had regained her dignity. "It's not what you think."

Libby took a sip of orange juice and lemonade. "I wondered what brought on your sudden enthusiasm for horse-riding. Where did you meet superman?"

Marina blushed. "We're just friends. I bumped into him at one of the Round Table dinners."

"Which you were attending with Henry?"

Marina swallowed a large mouthful of red wine. "My husband and Chester are friends, and Henry does Chester's legal work. He has business interests in the area."

"Looks like his interests extend beyond business."

"Don't be crude, darling." Marina pouted. "Chester just happens to ride at the same place. Henry knows all about it, of course."

"Of course he does." Henry, a slight, balding solicitor with an air of perpetual worry, never disagreed with his wife about anything.

Marina pulled out a selection of the pins that had secured her hair under her riding hat. "That's better. Anyway, you didn't come all the way out here by accident, did you? I know you, Libby Forest. You're on the trail of the poisoner." She shook her hair loose, raking her hands through the apricot waves. "I do hope it doesn't turn out to be that teenager lodging with you. She's such a pathetic little thing. So pale and gloomy-looking. She might have forgotten to wash her hands after taking drugs, or something."

"Mandy doesn't take drugs. Well, not in my house, anyway."

Marina sighed, theatrically, took a pair of silver earrings from her bag and slipped them with ease into pierced ears. "You'll be getting a reputation as a collector of lame dogs, if you're not careful. Like Bear and Max Ramshore."

"Max is no lame dog."

"Well, not exactly I suppose. Still, he'll let you down, believe me. Don't trust him, or Joe."

If Libby wasn't careful, Marina would be spreading gossip about her. "Max is hardly more than an acquaintance of mine, I promise you."

"Exactly." Marina beamed, triumphant. "Just like Chester and me."

Libby gave up. The food arrived and she took a deep breath of garlic and parmesan cheese. "Mmm. This pasta smells good. Do you often come here?"

"Sometimes." Libby would be willing to bet Chesterton Wendlebury had intended to join Marina for lunch today. What was really going on between them? Not that it was any of Libby's business.

She swallowed a delicious mouthful. "You told me something about Kevin Batty."

Marina tucked in to ham, egg and chips with enthusiasm. So much for trying to get fit. "He was a frightful man."

"You said he was a client of Henry's."

"Did I? Oops." Marina touched a finger to her lips. "Silly me. I'm not supposed to talk about Henry's work, but it's so difficult to remember what I'm not supposed to know."

"Tell me about Kevin, anyway. It could be important. The poor man's dead, so I don't think client privilege counts anymore."

Was that true? Libby had no idea, but Marina was satisfied. "Henry deals with corporate law, mostly. Firms who want to merge or take each other over. Utterly boring." She waved a fork in the air.

"He was writing contracts for a London company planning to buy land in Bridgwater. The land they wanted belonged to Kevin's father. He used it for plant nurseries, but they were hopelessly full of weeds." Marina's eyes glinted. "Kevin's father used to drink." She drained her own glass, not seeing the irony. "Six large bottles of cider a day, that's what I heard. No wonder he let the land go to ruin."

"Kevin didn't run the business?"

"Not then. He was just his dad's messenger boy, lounging around drinking, and spending all night in the clubs in Bristol. Until he found the company was offering mega cash for the land, that is. Then, Kevin jumped at it and tried to persuade his dad to sell. They had a flaming argument and Kevin's father had a stroke."

Marina lined up her knife and fork on the empty plate and looked round. "Where's the waitress? I think I deserve pudding, don't you?" A harassed girl with a pony tail scurried across the room, eager to please. Marina scanned the laminated list, ordered spotted dick, and turned back to Libby. "Now, where was I?"

"Mr Batty's stroke."

"Oh, yes. It wasn't Kevin's fault, but it gave him a shock. He inherited the business, cleaned up his act, refused to sell any of the Batty land and started making money by subletting to local farmers. He was worth a fortune, in the end."

"What happened to the London company? Did they buy land somewhere else?"

"Disappeared back to London, I believe. Henry said they'd expected the yokels down in Somerset to be a pushover, and to get the land for half what it was worth."

Libby kept her voice casual. "Do you remember the name of the company?"

Marina tapped manicured nails on the table. "Let me see. It was a string of letters. "ACT Ltd., or PMQ, or something."

The initials meant nothing to Libby. "So, Kevin turned out to be something of an entrepreneur."

Marina chased the last spoonful of custard round her plate. "Can't see that it has anything to do with poison in the sandwiches."

"No, me neither. Anything else you know about Kevin?"

"Nothing interesting. He was a bit of an old car fanatic, but so are half the men round here. He's a regular at the American classic car convention. It's part of the country fair. Full of Chevrolets and Pontiacs." Marina emptied her glass. "The fair's only a couple of weeks away. You should get your friend Max to take you."

"Maybe we could meet you there—with your friend Chesterton."

Before Marina could answer, the door of the pub crashed open. "You!" In the sudden silence, a tiny, red-haired woman wearing an anorak and battered wellingtons wove through the tables towards Libby. Every head in the room followed her progress. Libby froze.

The woman pointed a bony finger at Marina. "I saw your car parked down the road, Mrs Busybody. What have you been saying?"

Marina raised a dignified eyebrow. "I have absolutely no idea what you mean, Mrs Wellow, and I'll thank you to stop shouting."

The newcomer jabbed a scarlet-painted fingernail in Marina's face, leaned closer and hissed. "You told the vicar's wife my Theodore is no pure breed. It's a filthy lie, and he'll beat your Shipley into a cocked hat, come the show."

Marina, purple in the face, looked ready to explode. She rose to her feet, towering inches above her opponent. "Mrs Wellow, I'll have you know Shipley, whose kennel name is Wellington Shipshape, by the way, is a pure bred, registered springer spaniel." She gathered up her bag, lifted the orange jacket from its nearby hook, and tossed her head. "I will see you and your unfortunate mutt at the show." She swept regally out of the pub.

Libby resisted the temptation to applaud. Nothing would make her miss the county show, now. She paid the bill and drove home.

CHAPTER ELEVEN

Truffles

Libby returned to discover a neat list on the kitchen table, with the heading, "Cycling club weirdos." Mandy had been busy.

She'd scribbled a note at the bottom of the page. *"Round at Steve's. See you there, later."* She'd even remembered to leave the address.

Fuzzy sat on the windowsill, two white front paws together. His unwavering gaze was fixed on the garden, where Bear was digging up every plant that survived his last visit.

The dog looked up, noticed the cat, and burst through the back door. Fuzzy stepped elegantly from her perch and drifted past, as though by mistake, heading for her bowl. *You're a tease, Fuzz.* Bear followed, to gulp down a pound of beef while the cat nibbled gracefully on a few morsels of fish.

Libby snapped the door shut, restricting the animals to the garden and utility room. They weren't getting anywhere near the kitchen. She'd applied for a hygiene certificate and the inspector would arrive in a day or two. Animal hairs were not welcome on premises where food was prepared for sale.

Libby found it easiest to think in her beloved kitchen, surrounded by grinders, mixers and racks of saucepans, the tools of her trade. As she weighed and measured, chopped and tasted, her brain busied itself with the poisoning of Kevin Batty and Vince Lane.

She knew a little about Kevin, thanks to Marina, but nothing about Vince. She'd no idea what linked him with Kevin. In any case, how could the killer be sure he'd targeted the right people? So many had been poisoned, but only two had died. Not everyone in the cycling club would have eaten the same things. There were plenty of different sandwiches, not to mention chicken, tuna, and egg salads, as well as Libby's cakes.

She poured chocolate into moulds, moving mechanically. If everything was equally infected, why had only Kevin and Vince died? How was it managed?

Libby pulled containers from the new, dedicated fridge that had taken the last of her savings. She tore down the 'Poison' sign on the door. She'd laughed when Mandy stuck it on, last week. It wasn't funny now.

Squirting coconut cream, lemon mousse, and champagne truffle fillings into chocolate cases took all Libby's concentration. With a defiant swirl, she finished the final confection, loaded up the dishwasher, and checked on Bear and Fuzzy. They were snoring, limbs tangled, in their favourite apple crate.

Libby took Mandy's list up to her study. Most of the names were familiar. She found an Eddie Batty. Was he some cousin or uncle of Kevin's? Marina had said the area teemed with Battys.

There was Henry, Marina's husband. Libby paused. How much did he know about Marina and Chesterton Wendlebury? *Don't be nosy*. It was none of her business, really. Further down the list she found Vince Lane, Joe Ramshore, Simon Logan, and Alan Jenkins, the garage owner who nurtured Libby's treasured Citroen.

Mandy had scribbled notes in the margins. Apparently, Eddie Batty was divorced from someone called Sarah, who'd remarried and was now Sarah Smith. Eddie's new wife was Christine, previously married to Vince Lane. That was the first link Libby had found between the two men, but it was pretty remote. She dropped the paper on her desk. Almost everyone in Exham seemed to be related to everyone else, by birth, marriage or divorce.

A list of new emails popped up on the computer. Max's name stood out and Libby clicked. *Just to let you know I might be off the grid for a few days.* She snorted. It sounded like an episode of Spooks.

Her eyes slid down the email. *Hope you're being careful. I've been in touch with Joe and he tells me the bakery's closed. Let me know if you need anything.*

I met someone today who used to know your husband. He asked if you were living in Trevor's house in Leeds. You didn't mention you had a house up there.

Libby bit her thumb nail. Ali's house, left by Trevor, was in Leeds. A familiar, Trevor-related ache pounded the side of Libby's head. She closed the laptop, fished aspirins from a desk drawer and washed them down with a handful of lukewarm tap water. She was looking forward to her trip to Leeds, but first it was time to visit Mandy's friend, Steve.

***

Loud music told Libby she was at the right house. It drowned out the bell, so she banged the door with her fist. The next door in the terrace opened and an elderly woman peered out, spectacles on the end of her nose. "They'll never hear you with that racket going on." She stumbled down the path, through Steve's gate and up to the door, hammered on it like thunder, leaned down and bellowed through the letter box. "Oi. You've got a visitor." Without another word, she shuffled back the way she'd come.

Mandy, cheeks flushed, hair in spikes and mascara smudged, opened the door. Libby stepped inside, straight into a small living room. She recognised a sweetish smell that hung in the air, and sniffed, ostentatiously. "Are you high, Mandy?" The girl just giggled. If Steve was in the same state, Libby wasn't going to get much sense out of him.

A tall, thin teenager leaned, swaying slightly, against the door. Black hair, back-combed into stiff points, topped a face even paler than Mandy's. He must be Steve. A dragon tattoo climbed from the neck of a sleeveless black t-shirt. The boy's exposed arms were scrawny, his eyes half-closed, pupils dilated.

Libby took her time, letting her gaze roam round the room. The boy shifted from one foot to the other. When she thought he was uncomfortable enough, Libby said, "I suppose your mother's out. I can't imagine she lets you smoke pot at home."

The boy stared at the ground as he muttered, "She's at the Bingo."

"Then, I suggest you get rid of the evidence." Libby pointed at a jumble of cigarette papers, matches, and tins that she guessed contained something more exotic than tobacco. "You'd better make yourself a cup of strong coffee."

Mandy giggled. Libby would have something to say to the girl when they got home. For the moment, she kept her attention on Steve. "I thought Goths were supposed to be depressed." The boy mumbled something she couldn't catch. "I beg your pardon?"

He sighed. "I said, not real ones. Just the posers and losers who do Goth 'cos they don't have any friends. They're the ones all over the internet."

"So, where do real Goths hang out?" Interested, despite herself.

"Clubs, mostly. And record shops." Steve pushed himself away from the wall. "I'll get the coffee, I s'pose."

Libby glared at her lodger and Mandy stopped giggling. "You won't tell Mum, will you?"

"Not if you calm down and stop being so stupid. What were you thinking?"

Mandy tossed her head. "It doesn't do any harm."

"Well, we need to get some sense out of Steve." The boy returned, balancing mugs, and handed them round with all the exaggerated care of a Victorian footman. Maybe he hadn't been as high as he'd pretended. Libby said, "Where did you go to school?"

The boy hesitated. "Wells."

"Wells? You mean, Wells Cathedral School? Do they let Goths study there?"

Steve blushed. "I had a scholarship. Music."

"He plays the saxophone," Mandy chimed in. "He's in a band."

Libby ignored her. "Do you have a job?"

"I'm on a gap year before Uni."

"Oh? Where are you going?"

"Royal College of Music," he muttered.

A few pieces of information clicked into place in Libby's brain. Angela's husband was a musician. Exham was a close-knit community. "Steve, are you by any chance related to Angela Miles?"

"She's my aunt. She was married to Uncle Geoff."

"That's Geoff Miles, the composer?" Steve nodded, suddenly enthusiastic. "I'm playing in her gig in a week or two. You can come, if you like."

"It's a deal. Now, I want you to tell me what you know about this company that's trying to muscle in on the bakery."

The atmosphere froze. Steve fixed his gaze on the floor and mumbled. "What did you say?"

He heaved a heavy sigh and plucked at the frayed hole in the knee of his black jeans. "They're called Pritchards. My mate says the top man lives in some manor house in the Cotswolds and gets around in a helicopter, but he started out as a barrow boy in the East End of London."

"He's done well for himself, then?"

"My mate says he's crooked."

"Does he? Any evidence?"

Steve licked his lips. "He uses loopholes in the law to get businesses shut down, and then he moves on to their patch. Like when that tea shop in Riversmead had to close because it couldn't get a health and safety certificate. Pritchards bought up the premises and they're making a fortune. My mate says they paid off the inspector."

Libby murmured, thinking aloud. "Bribery's a long way from murder, though."

Mandy joined in. "What if they didn't mean to actually kill anyone, just make everyone in the cycle club sick. Then, the bakery would be shut down and Pritchards could move in."

"It's a bit extreme, don't you think? Exham's just a small place, not big enough for a huge concern like Pritchards to care about." Libby drained her mug. "How could they have poisoned the food?" She shook her head, dismissing the idea. "No, I can't believe a company like that would risk killing people, just to get a foot in the door in Exham."

Mandy looked disappointed. "But you never know."

Libby smiled. "No, you never do."

***

Libby left Mandy and Steve behind to tidy up before his mother returned. She took Bear for a final walk rounds the roads, promised him a trip out into the fields tomorrow, and returned home. She clattered ice into a glass, poured a hefty slug of gin and waved a few drops of tonic water over the surface, finished with a slice of lime and curled up on the sofa to think about Vince Lane.

He was almost as new to the area as Libby, and no one had much to say about him. Mandy said he'd sometimes worked at Alan Jenkin's garage. With the Citroen, suitably serviced, waiting for collection from the same garage, Libby had the perfect excuse to snoop around and ask questions.

Meanwhile, the thought of that house in Leeds nagged, like an itch Libby couldn't reach. Max had mentioned it in the email. Maybe he could help. She reached for her phone and dialled. Bear heaved himself up from the rug and rested his head on her lap. Libby scratched his ears.

"Are you busy?"

"No, actually I'm about to head back home. Business transacted, job done. What about you?" Bear's tail waved. He could hear his master's voice.

Libby swished gin round her glass. What exactly was Max doing at the moment? Had he just come from a shower, a towel round his waist, hair wet? Libby blinked to erase the thought and made herself listen. Max said, "I found out a bit about Kevin and his family firm. Seems he might have upset a few people over the land deal, but it was years ago."

"I remember something about it. Wait a moment." Max's phone clunked as he set it down. "Yes." He was back. "I'm looking at some of the paperwork."

Libby's mouthful of gin found its way to her wind-pipe. It was almost as though Max had known what she was about to ask. "Already? You've got it there?"

"On my laptop. Are you OK?"

"Gin went down the wrong way." She finished coughing. Now, he'd think she sat around drinking on her own every evening. She put the glass down. "Go on."

"The company he dealt with is called AJP Associates. They're still around."

That was a blow. "I was hoping it would be Pritchards."

"What do you think the P. stands for?"

"No. Seriously?"

"Seriously. Pritchards, known to be moving in on properties in the West Country, is part of the group that tried to buy Kevin Batty's land. I'll see what else I can find out about them. I should be back tomorrow."

Libby tried to ignore her stomach's tiny flip, not wanting to analyse her feelings about Max's imminent return. Would they quarrel again, or would their truce hold? "Listen, about that house in Leeds. Have you heard any more?"

"No, sorry, but I'll see what I can do. I'm sure it's nothing to worry about." Max's voice sounded odd, as if there was something he wasn't telling. He changed the subject. "How's Bear?"

"Listening to your every word." It was true. The dog's mouth gaped. Libby could swear he was smiling.

"Give him a treat from me." Max's voice took her by surprise. He sounded homesick, which was ridiculous as he was about to come back anyway.

Libby found she was smiling, as broadly as Bear. "I will. Come on over when you get here."

"Will you feed me?"

"Beans on toast?"

"Perfect." He was still laughing as the call ended.

CHAPTER TWELVE

Scrambled eggs

Libby yawned her way downstairs next morning, keen to retrieve her beloved Citroen from the garage and, at the same time, winkle tit-bits of information about Kevin and Vince out of Alan Jenkins' brain. She caught the whiff of fish. Mandy, in the tiny back room beyond the kitchen, emptied a tin of dog food into Bear's bowl. "And you've already fed Fuzzy," Libby approved. "I can smell it. You're trying to steal their affections." She'd let yesterday's pot-smoking go. Mandy was obviously on her best behaviour.

Bear finished his breakfast in three gulps and turned his attention to Fuzzy's. In the kitchen, toast popped up from the toaster. A pan on the cooker held scrambled eggs. "You've made breakfast for me, too?"

"I found a recipe online."

Libby sniffed the air, catching an enticing whiff of herbs. "Oregano?" Mandy nodded. "Smells good."

Mandy, her face pink, pushed across a piled plate and watched, face screwed up, as Libby took a mouthful, chewed and pronounced her verdict. "Perfect. Did you have a nice evening with Steve?"

Mandy's cheeks glowed. "I've said I'll go with him to his Aunt Angela's place today. The quintet are meeting to practice, though Steve says I have to call it a rehearsal."

"Geoff Miles's long-lost work. So, you're getting a taste for classical music. Is Steve playing the saxophone?"

"Clarinet. He plays that too."

"Talented young man. I'm going over to the garage to see if the Citroen's fixed."

Mandy spent an hour in the bathroom, finally leaving the house wearing a faux leather jacket, a size or two on the big side. Libby was sure she'd seen it on the back of a chair in Steve's house.

***

Alan Jenkin's garage appeared quite empty except for a single old vehicle whose pointed wings were an especially glaring shade of pink. Seeing no sign of Alan, Libby was about to leave when a spanner clattered on the floor, accompanied by loud and heartfelt curses. A long, grimy arm reached out from under the Cadillac, groped for and failed to find the offending tool. Alan Jenkins slid out, blowing on his left hand and muttering under his breath. He caught sight of

Libby. "Sorry about the language, Mrs F. Scraped my hand."

"Do you want me to clean it up?"

He grinned. "Nah. Happens all the time when you're around cars. Reckon the grease stops any infections." His hand, filthy with oil, was a mess of old scabs. A new cut slowly oozed blood.

"Shouldn't you have one of those pits so you can get underneath the cars?" Libby asked.

Alan grinned. "Where's the fun in that? There's one in the workshop, of course." He jerked his head towards an adjoining building. "That's where I work on your car. When I'm tending to this old lady, I like to do it here. You know, a bit hands on, you might say."

Libby struggled to find something complimentary to say about the car. "It's very—um—American." What did people see in these old wrecks?

Alan patted the wing of the Cadillac. "1969. She'll be at the show next week, if I can get her on the road by then."

"Is it—er—she your only old car?"

He wiped a greasy hand over his face, leaving a trail of oil, his face screwed up as though in pain. "She's not an 'old car', Mrs Forest, she's a classic."

"Sorry. She's lovely, of course. I just wondered if you'd had time to look at my Citroen?"

The frown deepened. "Course I did. First thing after I brought it in, I gave it the once over." Libby enjoyed special treatment at the garage. Alan owed Max a debt; something to do with legal advice when the garage owner stepped too close to the line. His gratitude extended to Libby. "What's Max up to at the moment, then?" Alan rubbed his hands with an old rag and stuffed it back in the pocket of his overalls.

"He's away. He'll be back tonight."

"Planning something special, are we? Going out for a meal?" Libby knew Alan's idea of a night out was a few jars in the pub and a kebab from the Greek take-away on the High Street.

Over in the workshop, the Citroen was buffed to a shine. "I can see my face in the bonnet." Libby sniffed, detecting the smell of polish. "But is the engine OK?"

"She'll stagger on for a bit, yet. A good goer, that's what she is."

"And this time, I want a proper bill. No discounts. Right?"

He shrugged. "If that's what you want."

"It is." She held out her credit card. "First, though, I want to ask you a few questions about the cycle club picnic."

Alan gazed at his feet, arms folded. "Yeah. Thought you might start on that. Bit of a private eye, aren't you?" She let the silence grow until Alan weakened. "Well, I was there when it happened."

"Were you? I didn't see you. Were you ill, too?"

"Nah, not me. Took my own grub, didn't I? The wife made up some cheese and pickle sarnis and a piece of pork pie."

"I never thought of pork pie as healthy eating, before."

Alan's brow furrowed. "Healthy eating?"

"Never mind. It was a joke. I'm glad you were OK, but I was really wondering about Vince. He's not been around Exham long, has he?"

"That's right. He's new. Arrived about ten years ago, when they opened that business park affair."

"You mean the place by the M5 with the hideous green warehouses?"

He grinned. "That's right. Vince drove a fork-lift truck." Libby bit her lip. This was no time for jokes about lifting forks. "He used to come down here of a weekend and work on the old girl with me." Libby deduced he meant the Cadillac. "Kevin came over, too."

"So the three of you were friends?"

The mechanic frowned, looking perplexed at the thought. "Suppose so. Used to do a day on the car, clean up and have a few drinks in the Lighthouse Inn of a Saturday. Vince used to keep on at us to go out to the clubs, but my wife wouldn't have that. Kevin went once or twice, I think."

"Kevin and Vince were both single, then?"

"Kevin used to be married, until Sheila ran off with the window-cleaner. Good riddance, he reckoned. Don't know about Vince. He might have had a wife once, but not living with him nowadays, if you know what I mean." He was frowning.

"You'll miss the two of them, won't you?"

"Ah. Reckon I will, at that. We had some good times."

Libby handed over her credit card. Alan grunted. "Yep, gonna miss old Vince and Kevin around here." As an epitaph, it didn't seem too bad.

***

Libby left the Land Rover outside the garage, to be picked up when Max got back from his mysterious, government affairs, and drove home to a quiet house.

She'd hardly hung her coat in the hall cupboard, when a white van drew up. She answered the door to a smiling Eastern European, who heaved a weighty cardboard box into her hall. "For Mrs Foster."

"Foster? That's not... Oh, Forest, you mean." Was it what she thought? Heart thumping, Libby grabbed a knife and ripped open the box. Yes. Her brand new cookery books.

She lifted out the top copy and laid it on the kitchen table with as much care as if it were a diamond necklace. A real book, with her name on it. She stroked the raised title on the front cover, ran her finger over her own name and opened it to the dedication. "To Robert and Alison."

She replaced the book in the box, sudden tears pricking the back of her eyes. If the bakery had been open, she'd have taken a pile of books in to show Frank and some of the customers. With Mandy out, Ali off on her own adventure in South America, and Fuzzy in the airing cupboard, there was only Bear to share Libby's achievement. "Come on," she said. "Let's have that walk."

CHAPTER THIRTEEN

Poisoned chocolates

Cheered by a long run with Bear in the fields, Libby put that moment of sudden loneliness behind her, humming as she lined her beautiful new books neatly along a shelf in the study. The doorbell rang again, but this time, Libby's visitors were solemn-faced police officers. Her mood plummeted.

"Mrs Forest?"

"You'd better come in." She offered tea. "Milk, two sugars?" The older one of the pair was Police Constable Ian Smith.

Arms folded across a round paunch, he eased himself on to a stool. "We've met before."

He'd been one of Joe Ramshore's team when Susie Bennett died. Libby forced a smile. "We have."

"Made fools of us all, didn't you?"

She swallowed. He wasn't going to make this easy. "I like to help the police whenever I can."

A brief smile flickered across the face of the younger officer, a slim blonde woman. "I'm Constable Sykes. Emily Sykes. We've just come from Sergeant Ramshore."

"Is he home, then?"

No one answered her question. Constable Smith bit into a hob nob. "This is a very serious matter, you know."

"Of course. Two people have died. It's a dreadful affair, but it's nothing to do with me, or the bakery."

"Now, I never said it was, did I?"

Libby looked from one officer to the other. Neither was smiling, now. "Am I some sort of suspect?"

"We're just making inquiries." Constable Smith looked around the kitchen, shrewd eyes noting every item. "Make cakes and chocolates in here, Mrs Forest?"

"Yes."

"Does your kitchen comply with health and safety regulations?"

She gulped. "The things I make here aren't for sale, yet. The inspector's due to come soon."

He scribbled in his notebook. Constable Sykes nodded. "It's a beautiful kitchen. Did you design it?"

So, this was 'good cop, bad cop.' "Yes."

Constable Smith smiled, revealing a set of large, tombstone-shaped teeth with a gap between the front pair. "But there were chocolates at the bakery." Libby's heartbeat raced. "Were they yours?"

"They weren't for sale."

"The cycling club came in to the shop that morning, I believe." Libby nodded. "Did they eat any of the chocolates?"

"Well, yes. I mean, we were trying them out—Frank, Mandy and me—when people came in to the shop, and I think a couple of people had a taste…" Libby's voice trailed off, her mouth suddenly dry.

"I see."

Forgetting her intention to answer questions as briefly as possible, Libby added, "There wasn't anything wrong with the chocolates. I'm sure of it. I made them myself. They were samples. I'm starting a business…" She heard herself babbling, and bit her lip.

"Does Mandy live here?"

"She's my lodger."

"Does she come in the kitchen?"

"Of course. We often eat in here, and I've been showing her…" *Be quiet, can't you?*

It was too late. "Go on. What have you been showing her?"

"Just some recipes." Libby felt sick. She'd dropped herself and Mandy in a hole and she was still digging. They'd think Mandy might have poisoned the cyclists. "Do I need a solicitor?"

"Now, then, we're just trying to cover all the angles. Nothing to be worried about, but we might need to talk to you again." Constable Smith's suddenly avuncular tone did nothing to still Libby's nerves.

Her hands were shaking when the police left. Could the poisoning possibly have anything to do with her chocolates? She closed her eyes and tried to think back, to the moment when the cyclists arrived in the bakery.

They'd been talking about Libby and Frank's new partnership. Mandy had a champagne truffle in each hand. "Champagne to celebrate," she'd said. Frank bit the top layer of chocolate neatly from a coffee cream. "You either love a coffee cream or hate it," he remarked. "Me now, I love 'em." It was one of the longest speeches Libby had ever heard from the baker.

Kevin had been first to poke a head round the door. His little round eyes lit up. "Chocolates?" Mandy told him at length about the plans for the shop. Kevin leaned on the counter, much too close to Libby. Uncomfortable, she offered him a free sample. Next thing she knew, the shop was full of cyclists.

But, who had eaten the free samples? If only she could remember. *Wait a minute*. Mandy and

Frank hadn't been sick, had they? So it couldn't be the chocolates.

She groaned. What if it was just one flavour, though? The lemon meringue, perhaps. She'd had one of those and Kevin ate several. Head thumping, Libby sank on to a stool. She tried to concentrate through rising panic. *Come on, you're supposed to be an investigator.*

She had an idea. To rule out the chocolates as the source of poison, she needed to know who'd eaten which flavour. What's more, she had to find out before the police decided the chocolates were to blame.

One part of Libby's brain was shouting at her, telling her not to be irrational, but it was too late. She was sweating, her heart hammering. It wasn't just about the police finding out, any more, or what might happen to her. She had to know it wasn't her fault. She needed to be sure she hadn't killed those two men.

If only Max was here, she could talk to him. It would be all right. He'd find a way to prove it wasn't her fault. But, Max was away. There was no one else.

Wait. Simon Logan had been in the shop, had eaten chocolates, and hadn't died. Libby could find out which ones he'd sampled. He was so calm and in control. Even the thought of speaking to him made Libby feel better. He'd know what to do. Why hadn't she thought of him before? He'd made it clear he liked her.

How could she get in touch? Mandy would know. Mandy knew everybody. It took Libby three attempts to dial the numbers on the phone, her fingers shook so much. As Mandy answered, Libby gabbled, "Simon Logan, he was in the bakery with the cycle club. Do you know where he lives?"

"Ooh, Mrs F. You do fancy him, after all. I knew it. I said he was perfect for you."

"No, I don't fancy him." Was that strictly true? "Stop giggling, Mandy, this is important. I need to speak to him."

"Well, that's easy. He's here."

"Here? Where are you?"

"I told you. I'm with Steve at his aunt's house, rehearsing for the concert. Her room's got good acoustics, apparently, whatever that means. Simon's here too. He plays the violin."

"I'm on my way."

***

Angela lived in a small village, just outside Exham. The Citroen crunched up the gravel entrance and Angela waved from the window. "So glad you've come. Yes, let Bear come in. He's very

95

well-behaved." She took off her spectacles and peered at Libby's face. "You're rather pale."

"I'm fine, thanks. Still tired, that's all."

Angela patted her hand. "We wanted to get on with our rehearsal as soon as we could. Let me introduce you to everyone. You know Mandy and my nephew, Steve, don't you?" Steve winked. "Marina's here, of course, although she doesn't play an instrument." Marina never missed a social occasion. "And here's Chesterton Wendlebury. Have you met?"

Libby's hand was engulfed in Chesterton Wendlebury's warm grasp. "Delighted to meet you again, dear lady."

Angela explained, "Chester plays the cello. And here's Alice Ackerman, a friend of Steve's from Wells, who's helping us out on the viola."

Alice wore a very low-cut red T-shirt, skin-tight jeans and a winsome expression, and Steve was standing very close to her. Libby glanced at Mandy. Arms folded across her chest, eyes narrowed, she held Steve's friend, Alice, in a steely glare.

Libby extracted her hand from Chesterton Wendlebury's, "I'm sorry to interrupt you all."

His voice boomed. "Quite all right, my dear. We needed a breather."

Angela steered Libby to the back of the room. "Have a cup of tea while we finish, then we'll all have a glass of wine."

Libby whispered. "I had a visit from the police, just now."

"No wonder you're looking pale. Was it Ian Smith? He's always been a bully. No wonder he's still only a constable."

Desperate to talk to Simon, Libby had no option but to wait and listen to the rehearsal. The players stopped from time to time, to repeat a phrase or correct a mistake, and Chesterton called a complete halt at one point. "I've lost my place, sorry to say. Afraid I'm getting old." Libby had no chance to get near Simon.

CHAPTER FOURTEEN

Champagne

The musicians seemed to play for hours, until Libby thought they'd never stop. She ached with tension. At last, Chesterton declared himself exhausted, and offered everyone a glass of the ice-cold champagne he'd slipped into the fridge earlier. Angela dispensed cheese and biscuits while Bear squatted, alert for fragments of food to fall, ready to snaffle every tit-bit before it hit the carpet.

Simon handed a full glass to Libby. "Did you enjoy listening to our mistakes? I'm afraid age and lack of practice takes its toll. Chester and I are a bit past it, really. Most of the time I only teach, these days. Young Steve's very talented, though, don't you think? He'll go far."

Libby couldn't wait any longer. She abandoned small talk. "I wanted to ask you about that morning in the bakery. You know, the day of the cycling club picnic."

"I'll never forget it." Simon shook his head. "Two good people killed on a day out. I was one of the lucky ones. Hardly ill at all. Whatever it was, I hadn't had much of it."

Libby blurted out, "That's the trouble. I think it might all be my fault."

"You?" Simon's eyes widened. "What nonsense. What could you have done?"

"The chocolates." It was almost a whisper. "I'm afraid there might have been something wrong with them. I need to know which one you had. You see, I was ill, as well, and so was Joe. Kevin was in the shop with us. I'm not sure about Vince, because I never met him, but he might have been there as well." Libby's voice squeaked. She slowed down. "What if everyone who was ill had the same kind of chocolate? There were some chili flavoured, some with parma violet, and a batch of lemon meringue."

"And which did you have?" Simon's voice was very gentle.

"Chili and lemon meringue."

Simon frowned. Libby's heart thumped. He looked so serious. "Do you know," he said, "I think you're suffering from some sort of guilt. Survivor guilt, I think they call it. I had one of the parma violet chocolates and I was fine. Of course there was nothing wrong with them. They were wonderful, by the way. You're a very talented lady."

Nothing wrong with the chocolates. The lump that had been stuck in Libby's chest had gone. *It wasn't her fault. She hadn't poisoned anyone.*

Simon was smiling. His teeth were very white and even, and his smile lit up his face. He was a most attractive man. Libby felt a delicious glow start in the pit of her stomach and spread through her body, until she knew her cheeks were flaming. It was a good job she was sitting down, for her knees felt wobbly. Simon leaned in. "Libby Forest, I'd like to get to know you better."

Libby bit her lips to keep from grinning like an idiot. Deliberately, she sat back and looked around. No need to seem too keen. Nearby, Alice Ackerman flicked a strand of hair behind an ear, smiled and turned her back on Mandy, speaking exclusively to Angela. "Steve gets his talent from his Uncle Geoff, I expect?"

Steve shook his head. He looked very young and earnest. He'd dispensed with the earrings and nose piercings, today. The girl went on, "I wish I had half his ability."

Simon murmured in Libby's ear. "Look at that young chap. Talented, young, not a care in the world: just like his uncle. Not surprised that Alice girl is keen."

Libby whispered, "Mandy's furious."

He laughed, his voice very musical. "All's fair in love."

Was Simon flirting? Libby changed the subject. "Did you know Geoff Miles, then?"

"Oh, yes, we were old friends. At university together. That's where he met the lovely Angela, of course, and cut me off, as a matter of fact. I'd had hopes of her for myself." Simon grimaced. He pointed towards the window. "Look. The sun's shining. Shall we take our glasses outside and make the most of it?"

Why not? Weak with relief that she wasn't the poisoner, with a glass of champagne acting on her empty stomach, Libby was in the mood to enjoy a bit of flattery from an amusing, intelligent man. She stood up. "It's certainly very hot in here."

Bear followed them out, velvety brown eyes never leaving Libby's back. She ignored a twinge of guilt. She was tired of Max's on-off approach to their odd, arms-length relationship. She owed him no loyalty. If only Bear wouldn't look at her like that.

They sat at a picnic table on the patio, surrounded by the scent of rosemary and lavender bushes. Libby raised her face to the sun's rays. Bubbles of champagne flooded her bloodstream, adding to the warm glow. Simon raised his glass. "Chesterton always has good taste, in wine and in women. Have you noticed the way he looks at Marina?"

Libby giggled. "They go riding together." She bit the inside of her lip. The wine was loosening her tongue.

Mandy had come outside, too. She leaned on the garden wall, watching. "Are you all right, Mrs F?"

The child was smirking. "I'm fine, thank you."

Simon held out a bottle to Mandy. "Can I pour you a glass of Mr Wendlebury's champagne?"

She shook her head. "I don't drink." Libby opened her mouth, about to protest. That certainly wasn't true. Mandy wouldn't meet her eye. What was the girl up to?

The patio door slid silently open and Steve ushered Alice through. She tripped over the step and giggled. Steve rolled his eyes. Bear paced back and forth across the patio. Simon watched. "Is there something the matter with your dog?"

"He's not mine. I'm looking after him for a friend." The dog whined. Libby called him over. "What's the matter, Bear? It's not like you to make a fuss." She scratched his head and he curled round her feet. "Did you feel left out?"

Alice stumbled to a patio chair and flopped into it, not noticing her skirt was caught on the arm. Libby looked at Steve. "How much did she have?"

"Just a couple of glasses." Steve shrugged. "Empty stomach, I suppose."

Simon's arm touched Libby's, warm through his wool jacket. "You played well, today, Steve. A chip off your uncle's old block."

"Oh. Right. Thank you. My uncle used to talk about you. He said the two of you used to be a team."

"We were, but Geoff was the one destined for great things." Simon lifted one shoulder. "Can't all be legends."

"Uncle Geoff said you were more talented than him, but..." Steve stopped in mid-sentence, blushing.

"But he said I wasted my ability on advertising jingles." Simon laughed. "It's all right. Geoff called it selling my soul, but I made a good living from advertising for a few years, before I went into lecturing. Geoff stuck to his guns. He wasn't rich, at first, but he wrote good music. You should be very proud of him."

"I am." Steve's eyes shone.

"It was tragic he died so young, just as his work was getting popular."

Steve said, "I was going to go to his concert. You know, the one that was cancelled the day he had his accident. Mum was taking me as a treat, because I passed my Grade Six saxophone. I remember everything about it."

"You were only young at the time. It must be ten years ago, now."

"Mum said Uncle Geoff was driving too fast..."

"I don't expect you know the story." Simon touched Libby's hand, glanced into the house and dropped his voice. "We don't talk about it much in front of Angela, because it was Geoff's own fault. He had a sports car. A Porsche. He'd had some sort of quarrel with Angela after the morning rehearsal, and he drove away in a huff, without her. He was going much too fast, as he always did, and he went clean off the road."

No wonder Angela hadn't told Libby. It would be hard to get over that sort of thing; quarrelling, then watching your husband drive away and never come back. "How dreadful. Poor Angela."

"Yes, she never forgave herself. Don't mention it in front of her, will you?"

Libby remembered the manuscript. "She was telling me about Geoff Miles's last work: the one you're all rehearsing. She said he was writing it when he sprained his wrist, and he could hardly finish it. I saw the writing: you could tell there was something wrong with his hand."

Libby broke off as Angela came through the doors, heading for Alice. The girl had left her chair and was swaying on her feet, humming quietly. Angela took her arm. "I'm afraid Alice has had too much champagne. Can someone please take her home?"

CHAPTER FIFTEEN

Thai curry

"Mandy, did you keep topping up Alice's drink?" Libby tackled her lodger as soon as they were home. She folded her arms, blocking the girl's route to the stairs.

Mandy didn't look in the least abashed. "She'll be fine, Mrs F. She didn't have that much champagne. She just can't take her drink."

"Don't look so smug," Libby scolded. At least Mandy knew how to stand up for herself.

Mandy giggled and shot a sideways glance at Libby. "I could see you were having fun with Simon."

"Don't change the subject. Anyway, it's none of your business."

"So, you don't mind if I tell Max that Simon was all over you in the garden?"

"Tell him whatever you like." It wouldn't do any harm for Max to know he wasn't the only fish in the pond. "By the way, Max is joining us for dinner."

"I meant to tell you. I'm going out."

"Steve?" No wonder Mandy was full of beans. "You really like him, don't you?"

Mandy's face was alight. She'd never looked so elated. "We're going to the club."

She disappeared, humming something tuneless. Libby pounded herbs into a paste and stirred coconut milk, lemon grass and lime juice in a frying pan, for a Thai curry. The exotic fragrance filled the kitchen.

The shower spluttered in the bathroom, reminding Libby she still couldn't afford to renovate it. *You can get used to anything.* She hardly noticed the orange bathroom tiles these days. They'd come with the cottage.

Drawers opened and closed, and hangers rattled. There'd be a mountain of discarded clothes on the chair in Mandy's room. She was a lodger, so there'd be no need to nag about tidying the bedroom. Libby hummed as she stirred. She'd enjoyed talking to Simon, and he'd looked as though he liked it too. She'd been sure he was about to suggest they meet up somewhere, when they were interrupted. Where was he most likely to take someone on a first date? A restaurant? Maybe that expensive French place that just reopened?

The wooden spoon was dripping sauce all over the worktop. Libby wiped up the mess with one hand. Was she seriously thinking about going on a date? Hadn't she given up all that sort of thing?

A phone rang. She jumped. Too much of a coincidence to be Simon, surely? She wiped her hands and ran to the sitting room to find the mobile. Would she say yes to him?

The phone's screen was blank. Disappointed, Libby stuck it in her pocket. How stupid. She should have recognised Mandy's ring tone.

What was that? Bear leapt up, barking, as a scream echoed down the stairs. Fuzzy hid under the sofa. Libby took the stairs two at a time, fear making her breathless. "Mandy? Whatever is it?"

The teenager sat bolt upright on her bed, tights round her ankles, leather skirt still unzipped. One shaking hand held a mobile phone to her ear, the other grasped the front of her t-shirt, fingers working, screwing the cotton into a ball. "I—I'm coming," Mandy stammered into the phone. "I'm on my way."

She dropped the phone on the bed and stared at Libby, eyes huge and black. "It's Steve."

"What's wrong?"

Mandy's thin frame shook so hard she could barely speak. Her mouth worked. "His motor bike," she whispered.

Libby took a long, trembling breath, determined to keep calm for Mandy's sake. "Is he—is he..." She couldn't put the worst into words.

"He's in a coma. In Mountview Park Hospital." Mandy stuffed a fist into her mouth, but there was no holding back the sobs that shuddered through her body. Libby squeezed her shoulder.

She had to get Mandy to the hospital. "I'll take you there. Put some jeans on. Oh!" The champagne! Libby couldn't drive all that way after those glasses she'd emptied. "Wait, I'll ring for a taxi."

With the phone at her ear, Libby had a better idea. She glanced at her watch. Max might have come home by now. She punched in his number. *Hurry up and answer, can't you?*

The phone clicked. "Libby, how did you guess? I just walked in the door."

Her shoulders sagged, tension draining away. "I need you to take us to the hospital, right now."

"What? Why?" Instantly alert.

"It's Mandy's boyfriend. He's been in an accident. We're at home and I've been drinking so I can't drive..."

Max cut her off. "On my way. Hold tight." The phone went dead.

Libby helped Mandy, shocked and trembling, to shrug on the leather jacket—Steve's jacket. She poured boiling water on a teabag, blessing her speedy hot water dispenser, added milk, and stirred in plenty of sugar. "Drink this while we're waiting and fill me in on what happened. Who rang you?"

"Aunt Angela. Steve was on his bike, on his way home. A car must have hit him, out near Middleton."

"Must have?"

"They didn't stop."

"Didn't stop? But that's..." Libby bit back the words. No point in upsetting Mandy even more. But why hadn't the car stopped? It was unforgivable. The driver would surely know if he'd hit Steve's motor bike.

The catlike purr of an expensive engine took them outside. Libby hadn't seen the Jaguar before. Max must have used a hire car from the airport. She felt a twinge of guilt. His Land Rover was still parked where she'd left it at Alan's garage.

The journey to hospital was a blur. Mandy sat in silence on the back seat, kneading tissues into damp balls. Libby filled Max in on the sketchy details she knew. "Who'd leave the scene without stopping?"

The hospital smelled of disinfectant. Libby's stomach contracted. No wonder people hated these places; chilling worlds full of strange noises, preoccupied nurses and weary doctors. They threaded through the corridors. A cheerful, buxom lady with round glasses and a volunteer's badge pointed them towards intensive therapy.

Angela had already arrived with her sister-in-law, Steve's mother. Angela wrapped Mandy in a hug. "He's just come out of surgery." That was good, wasn't it?

Mandy whispered. "Will he be OK?"

"We hope so."

Mandy sank on to a seat next to Angela and blew her nose. "I want to know who did it. I'll stay here for a bit, but you go, Mrs F." Colour flooded Mandy's face. "You find whoever it was, you and Max." She shook with anger. "The police will take forever, if you leave it to them, but you and Max can do it." If only Libby felt so confident.

Angela said, "Mandy's right. I'll look after her. Just do what you can, both of you."

Unsure, Libby glanced at Max. He raised an eyebrow and his head jerked, infinitesimally, towards the door. He was right, of course. There was nothing more to do here.

CHAPTER SIXTEEN

Coffee

The Thai curry was none the worse for waiting, but Libby could hardly taste it. Max laid down his fork. "I phoned Joe while you were banging around in the kitchen. He's home."

"And are you two talking, now?"

He looked thoughtful. "Strangely enough, we are."

"Maybe his near-death experience made Joe think about the things that really matter. You know, family and so forth."

Max wore an odd expression as he gazed at Libby, as though trying to see into her thoughts. "There's something wrong, isn't there, apart from Steve's accident? What is it, Libby? Is it your kids?"

Libby stopped pretending to eat. "Not exactly. It's just that I found out Trevor gave Ali a house. In Leeds. I didn't even know he owned one there. I just wish he'd told me." Libby longed to pour out her worries about Ali and the crazy dash to South America, but this wasn't the moment. She'd leave it for another time. Her daughter could look after herself, safely out of the way of the Exham poisoner. "It's Steve's accident that worries me. It didn't happen by chance, did it?"

Max walked to the window, looking out into the night. "Sometimes, good people get mixed up in bad stuff." He sounded worried.

"You think the accident was deliberate?"

"Sure of it. The bike was hit hard enough to tip it off the road and into the rhyne. Steve was lucky to be found. He could have been in the ditch all night. Whoever did it, must have felt the crash."

Max shook his head. "He could easily have died. I'm afraid that might have been the intention. The police are suspicious, too. Joe knew about it before I rang him. Ian Smith told him, I think." That was the constable who'd interviewed Libby. "They found paint on Steve's motor bike. They might be able to trace the car that hit him."

He smiled, but only his mouth moved. His eyes glittered. "You can relax, Libby, and leave this one to the police."

She wasn't going to let that go. "Of course I can't leave it to them. You're frightening me, Max. Don't you think it's time you told me anything you know? What's really been happening? Kevin, Vince, Joe, Frank's business, and now Steve. There must be a link between them, but I can't see it. Do you know what it is?" Suspicious, she went on, "I thought we were a team, but I get the feeling you're hiding things from me. What happened to Forest and Ramshore?"

Max's eyes were bleak. "I shouldn't have encouraged you. Stay out of it, Libby. People are getting hurt."

Libby breathed hard, thumping her mug down with such force coffee splashed onto the wood. "They're the people I care about. I want to help, and I get the feeling you know far more about what's going on than you're saying."

Max tapped his spoon on one hand, brow furrowed. "I'll tell you what I know. You already heard about Pritchards, the subsidiary of AJP Associates. I've been tracking them and their interest in Exham. All I can tell you at the moment is that they're big, rich and powerful." He shot a glance at Libby as if weighing up how much to say. What was that word that described his expression? Shifty; that was it.

"Is that why you went away?"

"Partly."

"Where to?" He dropped the spoon into his mug and stirred. The coffee must be cold, by now. He was giving himself time to think. *Can't you be honest, just for once?*

"I've signed the Official Secrets Act, Libby. I can't tell you more." Max heaved himself to his feet. "But, it's not enough for you, is it?"

He wasn't just talking about solving the murders, or Steve's mysterious road accident. He was talking about their strange, unspoken relationship. Libby pressed her lips together, biting the flesh with her teeth, anger fading, giving way to a cloud of depression, like damp fog. She felt her body slump. She couldn't bear lies and secrets. Trevor's betrayal had been more than enough for one lifetime. Libby needed, above all, to trust people.

It was her own fault. She could see, now, that she'd been expecting too much of Max. Deep down, despite all the denials, she'd been hoping something more would come of their odd friendship. Well, more fool her. She pulled her shoulders back and thrust out her chin. She was perfectly capable of solving the puzzle of Exham's poisoning and the attack on Steve, without Max's help. "If you won't tell me what's going on, you might as well leave now. And don't come back."

Max's face was suddenly pale under the tan. A lump formed in Libby's throat, and she opened her mouth, but it was too late. She couldn't take the words back.

He put his mug aside, neatly, on a coaster. "I'm sorry I can't tell you everything. I wish I could." He stood up. "Maybe this wasn't such a good idea. Come on, Bear. Let's get home." The dog leapt to his feet and Libby felt abandoned. Even Bear seemed happy to leave her alone. Seconds later, both Max and the dog had gone.

Determined not to cry, Libby wandered round the suddenly quiet house, fiddling with cushions and curtains. She tried to stoke up the ashes of her anger. How dare he? She'd show Max Ramshore. Frank was in trouble, Steve was at death's door, her own business was in jeopardy, and her husband had double-crossed her. If Max thought she was going to stay meekly at home, he had another think coming. She could put the jigsaw pieces together without his help.

With Trevor's strange deception in mind, she made more strong, black coffee, pulled out a file that contained the solicitor's paperwork, sent after the estate was wound up, and flicked through it all for the hundredth time. Surely there must be some evidence of houses in Leeds.

Despite an hour's careful reading, Libby failed to find a single clue to explain what Trevor had been up to. She sat straight. There was one sure way to find out what was going on.

Her phone dinged. It was Mandy, texting to say Steve was in a medically induced coma, the doctors were hopeful and she was staying with Angela that night. Libby flicked the chain on the door and, alone and miserable, fell into bed.

CHAPTER SEVENTEEN

Leeds

It was still dark next morning, as Libby left home. The sun rose behind the Mendip hills, bathing the motorway in shades of salmon and peach. A flock of birds rose, briefly blotting out the sky. The newly serviced Citroen purred happily.

Four hours later, Libby's satnav led her to a detached, Victorian house on the outskirts of Leeds. She drove past, assessing. The paintwork was neat, the windows clean, with bright curtains tied back at the side.

She checked the house number and, suddenly nervous, made her way up a short flight of steps, to the dark blue front door. A column of four bell buttons ran up the side, a name slotted next to each one. The house was divided into flats.

Libby held her finger on the lowest bell, belonging to an A. Grant. No one came. She tried the next, J. Brown, and drew another blank. The occupants must be at work. Or maybe they were students, still asleep. No, not students. The curtains were too tidy.

The top bell brought footsteps, faint at first, then louder. At last, the lock rattled and the door opened. A young woman cradled a baby on her shoulder. Almost as young as Ali, she was beautiful. Free of makeup, her perfect English rose skin gleamed with health. Her eyes were enormous, deep brown, in contrast to the pale blond of her long hair. Her delicate, elf-like face, creased against the light, peered from the darkness of the passageway.

Libby glanced again at the name beside the bell. "Ms—er—James?"

"Yes. Do I know you?" The young woman frowned and shifted the child to her other hip.

"I'm Libby Forest." Libby watched the woman's face, expecting guilt or embarrassment. It betrayed only mild surprise. If this woman was Trevor's secret mistress, she was also a brilliant actress.

"I'm so sorry for your loss," she said. "Please come in. I'm Tina, and this is Kyle." Libby followed her up the stairs. "I'm afraid my husband's at work at the moment." Libby felt a weight lift from her shoulders. She could easily deal with one woman and her child. Tina went on, "We were wondering what would happen about the house. Were you wanting to go through the accounts?"

Libby shrugged and cleared her throat. "Yes, please. It's taken a while to sort things out. Once I've dealt with the house, I'll be able to wind up my husband's affairs."

Tina glanced back. "Your husband?" Her voice lifted at the end of every sentence, so Libby wasn't sure if that was a question.

"Mr Forest, my husband."

The woman's brow cleared. "Oh, we were expecting his daughter. This house is in her name. Still, the others..." She left that thought hanging and went on up the stairs. Libby's brain raced. Others? The letter mentioned a house for Robert. Were there more?

Tina reached the top of the house. Libby let her do the talking while she caught her breath and vowed to get fitter. "We keep everything in the study." Tina led them through a green painted door into a wide and sunny apartment, simply furnished.

Tina set Kyle, a round mini-me with his mother's hair and eyes, into a complicated stand that allowed him to sit in the middle of a kind of carousel of toys, where he fiddled, banged and gurgled happily. Tina left the room, returning in seconds with her arms full of files. "Do you want to look at these while I feed Kyle? Cal, my husband, deals with all the properties."

Libby smiled, hiding the shock that made her hands shake. How many houses had Trevor owned? She took a deep, steadying breath. "How old is Kyle?"

"Just six months." The baby could be Trevor's, the voice in Libby's head whispered. The missing husband could be imaginary. Don't trust this woman. She seemed to know more about Trevor's affairs than Libby had ever done.

Tina put a stack of files on the dining table at the far end of the room, near the bay window. Silently, Libby spread them over the surface, wondering what she should look for. *AJP Associates*. The name jumped out. Pritchards was part of AJP. Pritchards, the company that tried to buy Kevin's land; that wanted to get their hands on more shops in Somerset.

Libby flipped a glance back towards the woman and her baby, just in time to see Tina slip a phone into her jeans pocket. Suddenly wary, Libby gathered up the files. "I'll take these away, if I may, Mrs James."

"Oh," the woman's face coloured. She looked round the room, distracted, seeming to search for a reason to object. "Why don't you have something to drink first? I don't think..." The door flew open, saving her from thinking.

A burly man, gorilla hands held close to his sides like a gun fighter in a western, burst into the room. Libby jumped up, files clattering to the table, gripping the back of a chair as two more, bigger, meaner-looking apes followed. "What's going on 'ere, then?"

Tina nodded towards Libby. "She's Mrs Forest."

The man sneered. "Well, I never. And what brought you here?"

Libby licked dry lips, using every ounce of will-power to stay calm. "I—er—I gather this is my daughter's house."

"Do you now?"

A familiar voice sounded from the doorway. "That's right."

Libby spun round. "Max?"

Max ignored Libby and held out a hand to the gorilla. "Mr James. We meet again."

The gorilla's eyes narrowed, then opened wide. "I know you. Why, you're..."

He covered the floor in two strides, to shove his face in Max's. Max smiled, not moving an inch. "Cal James, isn't it? Good to meet you again, although I fear you've been drinking. A bit early, don't you think?" He wrinkled his nose and stepped sideways, closer to Libby. "I haven't met your buddies, I'm afraid."

"Oh." James turned and waved his hands at the two heavies by the door. "All right, boys, Mr Ramshore won't be giving us any trouble."

Max took Libby's arm. She let him lead her back to the table. He said, "We need to talk about these files that your wife has very kindly produced. I see you've met Mrs Forest, by the way. Trevor Forest's wife. As you can see, she's a little surprised. She didn't know of your existence, or anything about the work you've been doing for her husband. I think it's time we let her into some of his secrets, don't you?"

CHAPTER EIGHTEEN

Tea

"Before we begin, Cal," Max said, "and in case you had any thoughts of getting rid of me, or Mrs Forest, I'll just warn you my colleagues are outside. I only have to press one button on my phone, and they'll be with us." His head jerked towards the window. "At the moment, they're enjoying McDonald's best in that blue BMW on the other side of the road."

Cal James reached the window in two strides. He swore. Libby wracked her brains, trying to remember if she'd seen the BMW on the motorway. No. She hadn't noticed a thing. So much for her skills as an investigator.

The gorilla grunted. "Me and the wife, we don't know nothing about anything. We just take the rents. For a fee."

"And a nice, fat fee, I expect." Max leaned back, the picture of relaxation. The two goons stood squarely in front of the door.

Max patted a chair. "Now, sit down and get comfortable. This might take a while. Maybe your wife, or girlfriend, or whatever, will offer us a nice, soothing cup of tea. And we won't be needing your two friends." His voice was as smooth as silk, but steel lay just beneath the surface.

Cal James dismissed the goons with a shrug and a wave. Their footsteps clattered down the stairs and the front door banged.

"I suggest you show me what's been going on before I send for my colleagues. You'll get credit in court, if you tell me what I need to know." Max took his phone out of his pocket and laid it on the table, switching it to record. "Start talking, Cal. Things might not even get as far as a charge, if you're helpful enough. Who knows?"

Libby sat on both hands to keep them from trembling. She hardly recognised Max. For a second, face rigid, he looked directly at Libby's face, and one of his eyes twitched. The wink came and went so fast, Libby could hardly believe she'd seen it. She sat up straighter and squared her shoulders. She could play it cool, too. Her hand was steady as she sipped strong orange tea.

Max settled at the table, opening one file after another. "Libby," he said. "I know a little more about Trevor than I mentioned when we talked yesterday." She squirmed, the quarrel clear in her memory. Max went on, "We've been looking into his affairs for a while, now. He owns several properties."

125

"That's right." Cal James grinned, showcasing a missing front tooth. Libby managed not to flinch.

Tina played with the baby, her lovely face betraying no interest in her husband's business. Behind that beautiful exterior, there seemed to be very little brain. Libby smiled at Kyle. Poor baby, with these two for parents.

"Now, to business." Max slipped off his jacket, hung it on a chair and rolled up his sleeves. "All we need from you, Cal, is a run-down of the properties, plus the names and addresses of anyone involved in buying and managing them. Easy enough, isn't it? Start by showing Mrs Forest where the rent goes."

An hour later, Libby's head reeled. Her husband had owned more than a dozen properties. He'd put two of them in his children's names. They, and others, were rented out, with hundreds of thousands of pounds of rent money tucked away in a succession of different bank accounts.

Max locked the files in his briefcase. "Right, we'll be in touch."

"Wait a minute. You can't take everything. What do I tell...?"

Max's face was grim. "What do you tell your contacts when they find themselves locked out of the accounts? Not my problem, Cal. You'd better

126

start thinking. Now, shall I call my friends and get them to take you to a nice, safe police cell?"

Cal rose. Max took Libby's arm. "Come on, let's go," he drawled. "Thanks for the tea." His fingers bit into her skin. "Have you got your car keys?"

Stumbling down the stairs, Libby fumbled in her bag, feeling through tissues, lipsticks, pens and loose coins with trembling fingers. She finally located the bunch of keys. "Here they are."

She almost expected the Citroen to have vanished, but it was waiting where she left it, fifty yards down the road, as though nothing unusual had happened at all. They climbed in. Max snapped. "Get going. Fast."

Libby turned the key in the ignition, foot on the accelerator, over-revving the engine. It spluttered. Her heart pounded. She tried again and it sprung to life. Libby caught sight of the two apes in a dirty, unmarked van on the corner. "Won't your colleagues stop them following us?"

"What colleagues?"

"The ones in the..." Libby broke off, her insides sinking. "You mean, you were bluffing? You don't have any back-up?"

"Sorry. None at all."

The Citroen's wheels squealed as Libby pumped the pedal. They were getting out of there as fast as the car could take them. "Max, we could have been killed."

"Not by Cal James. He's one of ours. But the others were looking nasty."

"One of ours? One of our what?"

"Same team as me. It's OK," Max twisted to look behind, "I think Cal's managed to call them off. Here, don't forget your seatbelt."

Relief tingled in Libby's fingertips. "I think you'd better explain. Why did we have to make a dramatic escape, much as I enjoyed it, if Cal's in your *team*?" She laid a heavy emphasis on the last word. Max wasn't forgiven. Not at all.

"He's under cover and his wife doesn't know who he is. One of the heavies is her brother." It was true, the taller of the two, the least ape-like, had Tina's pale, fair hair.

Libby shook her head, trying to clear it. "Are we in danger?"

"You're perfectly safe. You don't know anything and the gang we're after will find you're just who we said you are; an innocent wife with no idea what her husband was up to. Now, let's get back to Exham."

"Where's your car? I take it you followed me up here."

"It's hired. I'll courier the keys to the agency and they'll pick it up. I had a feeling we'd be leaving in this very charming old tin can."

Libby's hands on the wheel had stopped trembling, but her voice squeaked. "Do I take it Trevor wasn't the nine-to-five insurance salesman I thought?"

Max shook his head. "I'm sorry, Libby. It's been a shock for you. I didn't know what to say, last night. You see, I found Trevor's name on some of the Pritchards invoices."

Libby drew a sharp breath. "Pritchards?" The company she suspected of being behind of the poisonings, had links to Trevor.

Max was still talking. "You told me Trevor put a house in Leeds in your daughter's name. When I found you'd gone, this morning, I put two and two together. I had a hunch you'd take matters into your own hands."

"You mean, you didn't trust me enough to tell me about my own husband?"

"I thought..."

"Oh, I bet I know what you thought. Poor little woman, mustn't upset her. So much for our so-called partnership."

Furious, Libby crunched the gears. Max looked straight ahead. Libby gave in. She needed to know the whole truth. "Are you going to tell me what's been going on, or not? Was Trevor some kind of Mr Big?"

"No, but he was part of a large-scale fraud."

Libby forced herself to sound cold and calm. "You mean, he was a criminal." She drove on in silence, digesting the news, piecing together all the little clues. All those years together, and she'd had no idea. She'd ignored Trevor's long days, supposedly in the office, the strict rule that his wife and children keep out of his study, his refusal to let her take any part in the family finances. All the time, he'd been a petty criminal.

She was glad she'd stopped loving him years ago, but she would never forgive him for involving Ali, by giving her the house. That must be part of the tax fraud. She thought of another angle. "Am I about to be in trouble? Will I lose my home?"

"No, of course not, but you won't receive any of the ill-gotten gains. You see, Trevor was laundering money for a gang. It went through several hands, including his, on its way to becoming legitimate. It started with the gang's profits from a variety of crimes. Stolen cars, for example."

"Wasn't that what Alan Jenkins got involved in?" Max had helped his old school friend, Alan, out of that mess.

"That's right. Through a series of intermediaries, the gang paid your husband, Trevor, an innocent-seeming insurance salesman, to buy houses. He'd rent them out for a while, then sell them on and buy some more. The money, almost untraceable, eventually found its way to drug cartels in South America. Pritchards, or AJP Associates, the parent company, seem to be buying up business premises as well as rentals, but we don't have nearly enough evidence to convict them of fraud, yet. We'll be working on it for a while longer before we move in."

Libby's mouth hung open. "The money ends up paying for drugs?" Exotic drug barons seemed a million miles away from Trevor, her self-righteous husband.

"Drugs which are then imported to the UK, among other places. It's the biggest business on the planet."

Libby thought it all over as she drove. She could understand Max's refusal to tell her what was going on. He was worried she wouldn't keep it to herself. But they were partners. He should at least have told her everything he knew about her husband.

She glanced sideways. Max's face was blank, attention fixed on the road ahead. She was glad they were nearly home. His voice was polite and formal as he unfolded his body from the car. "I'll need to keep the files, but I'll get back to you if I find anything legitimate you can access. Maybe there'll be a little to fund your new business, but most of it is laundered money."

Safely home, Libby poured a large glass of red wine and drank it down in one draught. The truth was, she could trust nobody. Trevor and Max had each taken her for a fool, in their different ways. She'd imagined she was the one doing the detecting, but all the time she was missing clues about her own husband. A dark pall of failure settled over her, and the ground seemed suddenly to have shifted, like sand on the beach.

The kitchen had become Libby's haven. She ran her hand over the small pile of cook books on the counter top. She'd been so proud of them, but the excitement of becoming a real, published author had long since drained away. She clutched the wine glass until the stem was in danger of snapping and picked up the bottle, about to refill her glass.

She stopped, the bottle held aloft. How was Steve? She'd hardly spared a thought for the boy all day, and her phone had been turned off. She dragged it from her bag and pushed the switch. There was a message waiting from Mandy. "Steve still in coma but no worse. Frank in jail."

CHAPTER NINETEEN

Tomato soup and Dundee cake

Sleep was impossible that night. Alone in the house, tossing and turning in bed, Libby listened to the first drops of rain that tapped on the roof and clinked on the windows. At last, she gave up the unequal struggle with sleep and wandered downstairs, made a cup of hot chocolate and, wrapped in a duvet, watched old films until daylight.

At last, the clock hands scrolled around to a sensible time for visiting the police station. Libby fed Fuzzy, showered in the ugly green and orange bathroom, dabbed mascara on her eyelashes, swiped lipstick across her mouth and shrugged on her old parka. She wished she had Bear with her. Her eyes filled. She'd made up her mind to have nothing further to do with Max Ramshore, and that meant no more contact with the dog.

The police station was unwelcoming, the seats in the entrance covered in cold terracotta tiles. Libby finally diverted the civilian receptionist's attention from sorting piles of paper, asked to see Constable Smith, and settled down for a long wait.

"Mrs Forest."

She jumped. She'd been there less than five minutes. "Joe? You're back at work already?"

"As you see. Have you come to confess?" Joe's pallor and the dark rings under his eyes gave him the look of a tired child. Libby was on the verge of offering to take him home and make him tomato soup. "Or maybe you've seen the wrong side of my father." Joe offered a tight smile.

Pulling herself together, Libby followed him meekly through doors that clanged, down an open-plan office. Rows of police officers glanced up from computers, registering little interest as the pair passed through. At last, they entered a tiny room at the back of the building. "Your office?"

Joe blew air through his lips. "Not important enough for my own office. This is an interview room."

Libby examined the room. "No microphones or cameras?"

"Not here. Informal discussions only. You're not really under suspicion, Mrs Forest. No motive. Although," he went on, "plenty of means and opportunity. Working in the bread shop, you could poison the whole town if you wanted."

She ignored that. "Then, if you don't suspect me, maybe you could call me Libby?"

He let the ghost of a smile pass over his face. It was gone in a fraction of a second. "Well, then, Libby, how can I help you?"

"I hear you've arrested Frank for murder, but I can't believe anyone would think he's a killer. He's such a lovely man."

Joe leaned back, gazing at the ceiling. It was a dirty yellow, undecorated since the days when smoking was allowed. His gaze moved to Libby's face. "I can't tell you much, Mrs—er—Libby, but since you helped us out over that last business, I'll give you what I can."

A tiny grin tugged at Libby's mouth. This was the first time anyone from the police had admitted she'd helped solve last year's murder at the lighthouse. She bit her lip. She didn't want to annoy Joe. He was explaining. "The thing is, unlike you, Frank does have that all important motive, which means he has the full set; means, opportunity and motive. Easy enough to put digitalis or digitoxin, or whatever the men in white coats call it, in the sandwiches, or the cakes. Or even the chocolates." Libby beat down a familiar twinge of guilt. *It wasn't the chocolates. He's just tormenting me.*

Joe's barely-there, enigmatic smile made Libby think of his father. "Anyone can get hold of the stuff, on the internet or from prescription medicines for heart problems. Frank's old mother's taken one called Digoxin for years."

He tipped his chair forward, leaning both elbows on the table so he could look straight into Libby's face. "Frank has a ready-made source of the poison and every chance of tossing it in the bread or cake mix." He was enjoying this a little too much. He went on, "Kevin Batty did the dirty on Frank."

"I know. They had a quarrel over the price of flour, but that was years ago."

Joe's face fell. She'd managed to steal his thunder. "As it happens you're right, but so far it's the only motive we've got."

Libby wouldn't leave it there. "It's a pathetic motive. Why leave it so long to get revenge? You've decided Frank's guilty, and you're not even looking at other people. What about big business, for one thing? Pritchards are trying to take over premises in the West Country."

Joe snorted. "Seriously, do you think a multi-million company like Pritchards would kill two people, just to get their hands on Frank's bakery? I mean, it's a nice shop, I grant you that, but I bet they could buy Frank out with their small change."

He was right. A bakery in Exham on Sea would be almost beneath Pritchards' notice. Libby kept a rein on her tongue. She couldn't share the information on the money laundering operation in Leeds. Max had probably told her more than he should, yesterday. She could see, now, how difficult it was to keep government secrets. Had she possibly been just the tiniest bit unreasonable towards Max?

Joe seemed to have lost interest. "Chief Inspector Arnold's satisfied we've got our man, so we'll be bringing charges."

The legs of Libby's chair scraped the floor, as she jumped to her feet. "Well, I never heard such nonsense in my life. Honestly, Joe, Frank's motive is no stronger than Pritchards'. What about Vince? Why would Frank want to kill him?"

Joe flapped a hand in the air. "Maybe Vince and Frank had some sort of quarrel as well. We don't know, yet, but we'll find out soon enough, don't you worry."

"Besides, why did only two of the cyclists die, while everyone else survived?"

"Maybe they both had a sweet tooth, so they ate more of the Eccles cakes. Frank would know that sort of thing. He's been feeding cake to Exham for years."

Libby raised her voice. "That's absolute rubbish, Joe. Are you going to let a man like Frank rot in jail, without even bothering to look for the real culprit?"

Joe fixed his gaze on the ceiling once more. "If you think you know better, Mrs Forest, by all means go ahead and prove us wrong."

"That's exactly what I shall do." *Arrogant man.* Libby marched across the floor, ready to sweep out. One hand on the door, she turned. "And another thing..." Joe still sat at the desk, rocking back, watching, both eyebrows raised. The angry words died on Libby's lips. She suddenly understood what Joe was signalling. *He knows Frank isn't guilty, but his boss has tied his hands.* Without another word, she slammed the door and left.

***

She revved the Citroen's engine hard and drove home in record time to find Angela on the doorstep with Mandy in tow. A glance told Libby matters at the hospital were still bad. "Mandy needs to sleep," Angela said. Without a word, the teenager trailed upstairs.

Libby shrugged out of her coat and heaped coffee into cups. "You don't look much better, yourself."

Angela cradled her cup. "Steve's still in a coma. They're keeping him like that, to let his brain recover." The words, *if it can*, hung unspoken in the air. "Steve's mother's at the hospital now."

"Then, maybe you should go home, too, and get some rest."

Angela grunted. "I wanted to talk to you, first. I wondered if you and Max had got anywhere. You know, investigating?"

Libby finished her coffee, thinking hard. She couldn't ignore Angela's appeal for help, or Mandy's distress. If working with Max could help her find the murderer, Libby mustn't let pride get in the way, just because he'd kept things from her. The truth was, the two of them made a decent team. He'd once said, "People tell you things, Libby. You sit down with a slice of cake and chat, and before they know it, they've poured out all their secrets."

She made a pact with herself. From now on, she'd try not to fly off the handle every time Max annoyed her, but she'd keep the relationship purely business. Nothing personal. No more cosy evenings drinking wine and flirting, and no more stupid arguments.

Mind made up, Libby brewed more coffee and produced a well-matured Dundee cake. "Some of the things Steve told me might be important."

Angela let her breath out in a loud sigh. "I knew you were the right person to help, Libby."

"Let's not get ahead of ourselves." Libby couldn't share the information about Pritchards, or money laundering gangs, but she needed to know why they might be interested in Angela's nephew. "Maybe you can tell me more about Steve. What's he really like?"

CHAPTER TWENTY

Angela, Steve and Geoff

Angela put on her reading glasses, then took them off again. "Steve was musical from the day he was born. Geoff and I weren't able to have children, so Geoff was thrilled when his nephew started playing the recorder."

Libby screwed up her nose. She'd been forced to play the instrument at school. She's produced a regular series of high-pitched squeals, like a dawn chorus of cats, before her parents let her off the hook.

Angela went on, "Steve was only four. His mother, Geoff's sister Grace, and Thomas, his dad, were musical as well. That's how we all met, taking music degrees at University. Geoff would have been pleased as Punch to know Steve was going off to the Royal College and making a career in the business."

"Steve's quite a star, then."

She nodded, seeming close to tears. "We're going to postpone the concert, of course. It can wait a few months, until he's better. But, what if he dies?" Her hand covered her mouth, as if she wanted to take back the words. "You see, he's like his Uncle Geoff in so many ways. They both loved music more than anything, but they shared more than that. It's a touch of the devil, that's what my mother said when I married Geoff. Geoff could be wild."

"Like Steve." Libby thought of the drugs paraphernalia in Steve's house, the ripped t-shirts and the tattoos.

Angela frowned, making a strangled sound. She burst out, as if she couldn't hold the thought back any longer. "It would be too cruel if they died in the same way as each other, on the road."

Libby waited, as her friend gained control. Finally, Angela swallowed. "To be honest, Geoff's accident was his own fault."

"Go on." This didn't seem to be leading anywhere. Geoff died ten years ago, and Libby already knew about the accident. She wanted to hear more about Steve. Still, she'd hold her tongue, and let Angela get things off her chest.

"He loved music and fast cars, did Geoff. And, to be honest, sometimes he drank too much." Angela was twisting a ring on her wedding finger. It flashed, mesmerising, as she turned it round and round. "We were rehearsing for the concert. It was the same music we were playing the other day."

Angela gave a sad little laugh, more like a hiccup. "Geoff was angry with me, that day, because there was a mistake in the printing of the posters. I hadn't proof read them properly and his name was spelled wrong. We only noticed during that last rehearsal. Geoff was furious. He called me all sort of names. Still, I was used to that. It was just his way."

A rueful smile crossed Libby's face. She knew about ranting husbands. Angela went on talking. "He said I was to get it fixed and he'd go to the hotel for lunch on his own. He set off in the Porsche, as fast as usual. The road was steep and twisty, and he was so mad, he must have been careless. Everyone else followed him while I stayed behind, on the phone to the printers." She had to stop a moment, to gain control of her voice. "The others saw his car, upside down in the valley."

She paused to blow her nose. Libby asked, "Who were the others, who found him?"

"Oh, didn't I say?" Angela counted them off on her fingers. "Apart from Geoff and myself, there was Steve's father, Thomas, his mother, Grace, and Simon. We called ourselves the Circle of Fifths. They were all very kind to me. I don't know how I'd have survived without them. That's one of the things about music. It brings people together. The members of the quintet were my closest friends." Her eyes filled. "Not many of us left, now. Steve's father died last year, from cancer. Grace and I both gave up performing regularly, after Geoff died."

"So, Steve and Alice were the newest members of the quintet."

"That's right. Two very talented young people."

Libby murmured, "Have you known Alice long?"

"Steve met her at Wells. They're very competitive. Alice is really rather brilliant, at her other studies as well as music. She's off to Cambridge, this year." Libby breathed a small sigh of relief on Mandy's behalf. Her rival would soon be leaving the scene.

Angela rose and stretched. "Look at the time. I must have been here ages. And I hardly talked about Steve at all." She looked around for her scarf. "There's something I wanted to mention, though. When we talked about the manuscript, before, I said Geoff sprained his wrist while he was writing it. Do you remember?"

Libby thought back. "The scruffy writing?"

"That's right. Then later, I thought about it, and realised it was the wrong year."

"The wrong year? How do you mean?"

"He'd sprained his wrist the year before."

"And it had healed by then?"

"It must have, if he was playing the clarinet again, mustn't it? He was playing in the concert. I suppose he was just tired, and that's why his writing was so careless. He often took on too much. Didn't know how to refuse work."

Angela tied the silk scarf round her neck. "Anyway, I won't grumble, because he left me very well off."

Half way down the path, she turned back. "By the way, Marina rang me to remind me it's the spring show tomorrow. Are you going?"

Libby had completely forgotten. "Good job you reminded me. Marina told me about it, and I've taken on a stall."

CHAPTER TWENTY-ONE

Biscuits

A flicker of mixed excitement and terror woke Libby. Today was the spring show. It was a grand affair, apparently, the first she'd ever attended, with a wealth of competitions and exhibitions in the programme. The ploughing competition would take up three nearby fields, the year's best lambs would be on show in one ring, and the American classic car rally would cover half the rest of the show ground.

It was also Shipley's big day. The dog show was planned for the afternoon. No doubt Marina had risen early to shampoo the springer spaniel. Libby wasn't going to miss Marina's show-down with Mrs Wellow.

She'd spent almost the whole night preparing for her stall. The health and safety inspector had visited late yesterday, peered through wire-rimmed glasses into every inch of the kitchen, pursed his lips at the array of separate sinks and fridges, and, reluctant, as though it pained him, let Libby have the prized certificate. She could offer her wares for sale. Today she'd be letting children ice biscuits, hoping their parents would buy a copy of *Baking at the Beach* and maybe a bag of hand-crafted chocolates.

She drew back the curtains to find rain blowing horizontally from a uniform grey sky. Not a single inch of blue sky broke the monotony. Crazy, holding an outdoor show so early in the year. Still, her granny had always said, "Rain before seven, fine before eleven." Libby dug out her warmest waterproof jacket and a new pair of well-lined wellies. At least her stall was in a tent.

She loaded the car with tins full of product, boxes so weighed down with books she could hardly lift them, and piles of giveaway bookmarks. The Citroen coughed its way to the show site.

After three trips back and forth to the car, Libby spread clean white sheeting over her allotted table and unpacked her wares. "Morning, Mrs F." Alan Jenkins appeared at the door of the tent, almost unrecognisable in a clean waxed jacket and some kind of wide-brimmed hat. "How's the car?"

"Overworked, I'm afraid."

"You been driving her hard, then?"

"Just up the motorway to Leeds, but I don't like the noise in the engine."

He sucked his teeth. "What did I tell you? She needs gentle treatment. She's a lady, that one."

Bear appeared from nowhere, reared up, planted his paws on Libby's shoulders, and licked her face. She scratched the rough fur on top of the animal's head. Max, close behind, hauled the animal down, clipping on a lead. Libby glared. "Keep Bear away from the food on the stall, won't you?" She winced. She'd meant to build bridges with Max and be business-like, but she sounded plain bad-tempered.

"I heard you'd be here." He smiled, but the glint in his eye told Libby he was annoyed.

She flashed a synthetic smile. "Sorry, I've got to set up." She bent down behind the table, unloading books. Alan, with surprising tact, had melted away.

Max joined her. "I'm sorry I took you by surprise over Leeds. Won't you forgive me? Look, the sun's coming out."

Reluctant, she straightened up to look through the entrance to the tent. A tiny patch of sky had turned a slightly paler shade of grey. "Call that sun?"

"You wait. It's already drying up. Look, I'll even buy one of your books."

That was too much. Imagining Max, who ate takeaways or visited restaurants for his meals, attempting to bake a cake, Libby felt the corners of her mouth twitch. She offered an olive branch.

"Do you think I dare sell chocolates after what happened? I've got a hygiene certificate."

"Of course. If you don't, people will think there's something wrong with them. You know you didn't poison anyone. It's the bakery that's in trouble, not you." Libby straightened up. Her trestle table, neatly covered in white sheeting, decorated with red-ribboned, cellophane bags of chocolates in wicker baskets, was inviting.

The day wore on into an afternoon of watery sun. Mandy arrived, almost back to her old self after nearly twelve hours of sleep, and took over the stall for the afternoon. She settled down in a huddle of children and biscuits and stuck her tongue out. "Like my new stud?"

The last few drops of rain had dried up as Libby wandered outside. The dog show was under way on the other side of the park, and Libby could see Marina leading Shipley into the ring. Was that Mrs Wellow on a collision course with her rival? It was too good to miss. Libby began to run.

"Look out!" Something thudded into her chest and she fell, landing heavily on her back, every ounce of breath squeezed out of her body. Bear barked, paws on her chest, as with a flash of gleaming chrome, a car whizzed past, inches away. Libby scrambled to her feet, gasping.

A hand on her arm steadied her. "Idiot. Can't you look where you're going?" Max sounded furious. Bear whined, mouth open, tongue lolling.

Libby shuddered. "I think Bear just saved my life. Where did that car come from?"

It juddered to a halt, yards away, and Chesterton Wendlebury stepped out. "You almost went under my wheels, dear lady. Are you all right?"

Libby cringed. "That was stupid of me. Sorry. I'm perfectly OK. You didn't touch me."

A crowd was collecting. Max still held her arm. "I think you need a stiff drink." She nodded. Anything to get away from all those eyes.

Wendlebury slapped Max on the back. "Good idea, good idea. I'll park the old lady and join you."

A half pint of locally-brewed beer in hand, Libby found a space on a straw bale in the refreshment tent. Bear lay at her feet. She took a long gulp, glad of the warm, malty taste at the back of her throat. "I feel a fool."

Max laughed. "I'm surprised we don't have more accidents, here."

"What kind of car was that, anyway?"

"A Mustang Convertible. Made around 1965. It's one of Wendlebury's collection; he's got dozens of them. He takes them from one show to another. Alan's here somewhere, with one of his." He frowned into Libby's face. "You're sure you're OK?"

Libby remembered the conversation she'd had with Alan, a few days ago. "Several people around here have old cars—what Alan calls classics—don't they?

"Most of them are probably here today."

"Did Kevin Batty have one?"

"Used to. He spent hours fiddling around with it, him and Vince. They were mates." Libby said nothing. Her mind was too busy. She opened her mouth, then closed it again. She wouldn't tell Max, yet, about the idea she'd had. He kept things from her, and she could do the same.

CHAPTER TWENTY-TWO

Beer

"Are you sure you're all right?" Max still looked worried.

Libby forced a smile. "Sorry. I'm just embarrassed at making such a fool of myself. I was on my way to watch Marina do battle with Mrs Wellow at the dog show, but I think I'd rather stay here for a while."

Max's leg felt warm and strangely comforting against Libby's. He took a long draught of Butcombe Gold beer, taking a minute to roll it round his mouth. "Good idea. Listen, Libby, I wanted to apologise. I should have told you what I knew about Leeds. I'd no idea you'd go rushing up there in your old tin can. You could have been in real danger, you know. Don't do anything like that again, will you?"

Libby swallowed. "If we're still partners, Ramshore and Forest, we need to talk more. And we need to stop arguing and tell each other about ourselves. You know, personal things."

Max leaned over to pat Bear. "I'm not good at sharing."

"I've noticed. You've hardly told me anything."

"What did you want to know? You can ask anything you like."

"I don't want to be nosy." Max snorted. Libby tried to find the right words. "Look, I'll tell you something about me, then you tell me something about you. Something personal. How about that?"

He nodded. "Sounds fair."

"Well, you know my daughter came to stay?" Libby told him about the row with Ali, how devastated she felt when Ali told her she was leaving the country, and how she found the letter from Trevor. Tears started in Libby's eyes. "I never really understood Ali. She was Trevor's daughter, much more than mine, and now, I'm afraid I've lost her."

Max took her hand. "None of us get parenting right, but I think you said just the right things to Ali. She wanted you to know about the house. That's why she left the envelope where you were bound to find it." Libby sniffed and blew her nose.

"And now, it's my turn, isn't it?" He drew a long breath. "While we're talking about children, I suppose I need to tell you more about mine. I'm surprised no one in town's given away my guilty secrets." Libby waited. "I had a daughter, too. Ten years younger than Joe."

He cleared his throat. "When Debbie and Joe were growing up, I was in banking. Living in London, working all the hours in the week, I hardly saw the kids, or Stella, my wife. I meant well, of course. I had good intentions, and we all know what happens to them." He lifted a shoulder, looking suddenly unsure of himself.

"I thought I was doing the right thing, being a good husband. I made money. Plenty. We had a Hampstead house and a place in Italy, but I was never at home with the family. I didn't have time for holidays, or helping the kids with homework, or going to meetings at the school."

He emptied his pint glass. "It's a common story. Nothing special. Stella didn't need to work. She was bored, with nothing to do all day but go to lunch with her friends. I guess that's where she started drinking."

He balanced the empty beer glass on the hay. "I loved my kids, but I thought providing for them made me a good father. They had everything they wanted." He laughed, but it sounded harsh. "Joe hardly wanted anything. He was on the way to being a scientist. He used to run experiments in the garage. Debbie, though, liked having things. Clothes, toys, ice-skates. When she was twelve, she wanted a pony and like a fool I bought one. She kept it at the riding school."

"After a while, she stopped riding the poor thing and it began to get fat. I came home one weekend, and the phone rang. It was the stables, to say they were worried about the animal."

He shrugged. "I should have let Stella deal with it, but it was eleven in the morning and she was already well down her second gin and tonic. So, I became a hands-on dad and gave Debbie a good talking to." He shook his head. "I don't think I'd ever punished her before. I said we'd sell the horse, and I sent Debbie up to her room."

He reached into his pocket and pulled out a wallet, flipping to a photograph. "Here she is. She was a lovely girl. It was my fault she was spoiled."

Libby felt sick. This was leading somewhere she didn't want to go. She whispered. "What happened?"

"I bet you can guess. Debbie took no notice, slammed out of the house, caught the bus to the stables and took the horse out for a ride. On the road..."

Libby put a hand on his arm. "There was a crash?"

He nodded. "A lorry sped past, too close. Button, the horse, reared. Debbie fell off and hit her head. She wasn't wearing a hard hat. She died."

Max kept his eyes on the photo. "As you can imagine, the marriage didn't last long. I had an affair, and my wife found out. We divorced, Joe wanted to stay with Stella and I let him. I'm afraid I ran away from it all."

Max glanced at Libby, then looked away, eyes bleak. "I left the job and came back to Exham, where I'd grown up. I did nothing for a while but hit the bottle. It was Joe that saved me, oddly enough. One day, he arrived at the door with a degree, a girlfriend and a job with the police, and gave me a piece of his mind."

Libby could imagine. She glanced round, making sure no one could hear. "That's when you joined MI6 or whatever it is?"

"That's right. If Joe could make something of himself, so could I. But it's shaming to know your son's a better person than you, and I've been hard on him. When he was poisoned, I thought I was going to lose him, too."

No wonder Max had been short-tempered. Libby hung her head. If only she'd been less prickly, less worried about her own affairs, she'd have seen there was something seriously wrong. She opened her mouth, not sure what she was about to say.

Chesterton Wendlebury loomed above her head. "Well, it looks like you're in fine fettle." Bear growled. "I'll join you, if I may." The man smiled at Libby, showing his large teeth. "Seems to me you're a bit accident prone. Missed you by a whisker."

Libby smiled, forcing herself to be polite. Chesterton Wendlebury made her uncomfortable. "How did Marina get on in the dog show?"

"It's still going on. Thought you might like to go over there with me."

Max stood. "We'll all go. Should be fun." Libby slipped her arm through his. He gave it a small squeeze.

The judging was under way. Seven finalists paraded round the ring. Shipley had made it to the last few, alongside Mrs Wellow's Theodore. Marina and her diminutive, red-headed rival kept their eyes fixed on the judge, a dapper man with a shooting stick.

Finally, after walking round each dog amid much loud harrumphing, he made his decision, raised a hand, and beckoned Shipley to jump on to the winner's podium.

Mrs Wellow tugged on Theodore's lead, dragged him across to the front of the podium and jabbed a finger at Marina. "I told you what would happen." Her voice was shrill, reaching every ear round the ring. "A cheat, that's what you are. You've bribed the judge."

The audience gasped, thrilled. "Oh, I say!" The judge intervened. "You can't say things like that, madam."

"Can't I just? You watch me." Mrs Wellow spun round, to the audience. A camera whirred as the photographer from the local paper took a series of close-ups. "I'm telling you now, Marina Selworthy is nothing but a cheat. That dog of hers is no pure-breed. He only won because she's sleeping with one of the local toffs, and that's a fact."

Laughter rippled through the crowd. Marina gasped, one hand on her ample chest. "How dare you!"

"Now then." Constable Smith materialised from the audience and took Mrs Wellow's elbow. "There's no need for that sort of talk."

The red-head shrugged free. "You'd better watch out." Her outstretched finger followed Marina as she left the judging ring, head high, Shipley dancing at her feet. "I'll be getting my own back on you, just see if I don't."

***

Back at the stall, Libby counted the proceeds. "Do you know, I think we've actually made a profit." She handed Mandy a pile of notes. "Thanks for your help."

"I had fun." The teenager's face was flushed.

158

"You know, you're very good with children. Much better than I am." Libby put the last few biscuits back in their tin. "Do you know when Steve's coming home?"

"In a few days. The doctors say he'll be fine."

"He had a lucky escape." Libby chose her next words with care. She didn't want to frighten Mandy. "Have the police said anything more about the accident?" Mandy shook her head and Libby let it go. Poisoned cyclists, Steve's bicycle, classic cars, road accidents. She shrugged, and picked up a pile of empty boxes. There was a visit she had to make.

CHAPTER TWENTY-THREE

In the rhyne

Libby dropped Mandy at home, then climbed back in the car. "I won't be long." She knew plenty about Kevin Batty and his old feud with Frank, but Kevin wasn't the only victim of the poison attack. She still didn't know enough about Vince, Kevin's friend, the other cyclist who died. Why had he been killed, as well?

Libby pulled Mandy's list of local people out of her pocket. There he was. Vince Lane, with an address in a village out on the Levels. Mucklington. The name rang a bell. Libby concentrated. Ah, yes, the great floods had cut the place off from civilisation. Boats, floating up the main road, headlined the national news for days.

She fiddled with the satnav, turned the car and set off across the Levels, rewarded by miles of green fields that stretched out as far as she could see, criss-crossed by drainage rhynes. No wonder the cycling club loved their days out here. Libby wished she had Bear with her, today. He adored the freedom of the Levels.

She had a feeling she was getting closer to the truth of Steve's accident, but she couldn't grasp any clear link with the death of the cyclists. Maybe they were two separate events? She pondered that thought for a moment, then shook her head. She felt sure there was a connection, if only she could figure it out.

She glanced at the satnav. Mucklington was only half a mile away. She put her foot down on the accelerator, watching out for more treacherous bends hidden by withy, and soon found herself on the single road to the village. The surface was smooth, newly laid, the road raised several inches, no doubt to combat flooding. The fields of pasture nearby were bright with spring green and grazed by contented cows.

She drew to a halt outside a short row of terraced cottages, left the car and tapped on the door of number three. There was no answer. She tapped again, stepped back and looked up at the windows on the first floor. A single curtain dangled limply. Libby dropped her glance to the ground floor. There were no curtains, blinds, nor any other sign of life down there. She stepped closer, shaded her eyes with one hand and peeped through the window. A cooking hob and a sink were visible, but otherwise, the room was empty.

"They're gone." Libby jumped, startled, at the voice in her ear. An elderly man in a flat cap and brown overalls nodded. "Vince's wife left years ago, and now, he's a goner." The man laughed, and the laugh turned into a cough. Recovering, he looked Libby over and pulled off his cap. "I always thought his heart would kill him off, but someone got there first."

"His heart?"

The old man nodded. "Vince used to work on the farm over yonder, along with me." He jerked his head towards the field of cattle. "Farmer had to let him go on account of the heart failure." He sniffed. "On a mountain of tablets, he was. Only a young man, half my age. I used to come in of an evening. 'Vince,' I'd say, 'Vince, you need to give up the cider,' but would he ever? Not Vince. 'I'll go when it's my time,' he'd say. 'The cycling keeps me fit.' "

Vince's neighbour peered over Libby's shoulder into the house. "He was chairman of the cycling club, you see. Had been for years. When his heart was first playing up, they used to come round here often, to see how he was going. Every member of the club must have tramped up and down this path."

He nodded, lost in the memories. "Then, when Vince got better, they used to let him pootle along at the back on his old bike. We thought the cycling might give him a heart attack, but he wouldn't give up. It took a dose of poison to finish young Vince."

"Ah well." The old man put his cap back on. "Vince's time came quicker than he thought. This place'll be going up for auction, though who'll want to buy anything here, since them floods, I don't know. No value in these houses, not these days."

He shambled off. Libby, perplexed, wondered whether to knock on any of the other doors. She shivered. The place felt eerie. She gave in to temptation, got back in the car and began the drive home.

She slipped a CD into the car's ancient player. One of the benefits of independence was listening to music she chose herself, without husband or family rolling their eyes at her choices. Spirits suddenly high, she turned up the volume on the Eagles, singing along at the top of her voice to *Hotel California.*

She rounded a bend, hidden by a small outcrop of trees, and saw the front end of a Range Rover bearing down, only feet away. She wrenched the wheel to the left, skidded on a patch of mud, tried to correct and felt the car slide at a right angle to the road. Hands clenched on the steering wheel, she hung on as the front wheels lurched off the road, over a patch of grass and into the accompanying rhyne.

Libby flicked off the music and revved the engine. The front wheels spun helplessly, failing to gain traction, hanging over the ditch. She gave up, turned off the engine and unclipped her seat belt. Someone tapped on the window. "Chesterton?" Libby opened the door. A worried frown creased the familiar face.

"Good gracious me, m'dear. Not you again. Are you hurt?"

"Not at all. But I'm stuck." Chesterton Wendlebury, vast bulk clad once more in full riding kit, leaned over to squint at the front of the car. "We'll soon have her out of there."

He strode across to the rear of the Range Rover, threw up the boot and fumbled inside, emerging with a length of rope which he fastened round the tow bar. Libby stepped forward, hands outstretched. "Here, I'll fix it on to the car." *I'm not a helpless little woman.*

"Good heavens, no, m'dear. Let me do it. You must be shaken." Libby, exasperated, had no alternative but to watch impotently as he fastened the tow rope, climbed back into the Range Rover and drove off, slowly, smoothly, heaving the Citroen on to dry land. "There we are." Beaming all over his ruddy face, he untied the rope. "No damage done, I think. You'll be right as rain."

It was too late for indignation. It would be churlish to complain the Range Rover had been speeding, now its owner had rescued her. Libby forced a grateful smile and fluttered her eyelashes. Men like Chesterton Wendlebury liked woman to be helpless and weak.

"Now, no need to thank me," he went on, condescending. "Just be careful in future. These roads can be tricky when you're not used to them." He was standing very close and Libby found herself backing away. His smile was warm, his teeth large. "Look what happened to that unfortunate boy, Steven. I hear he's still very poorly."

Libby swallowed. "The doctors are hopeful he'll be fine." She watched his face.

"Good, good." The smile hardly changed. "Let's hope he's on the road to recovery, shall we? That little girl lodging with you, what's her name, Amanda, is it? She'll be relieved."

"Mandy. Yes, we all will." Libby looked around, curious. "Were you on your way back from the riding stables?"

He turned to stare back along the road. Libby moved to the door of her car and grasped the handle, the metal comforting in her hand.

Wendlebury went on, "Yes, had a charming ride with your friend, Marina." His eyes were back on Libby, as if daring her to comment. "On my way home to change, now. Back to business, eh? And what brings you all the way out here?"

She thought fast, reluctant to tell this man too much about herself. "I came out for a spin to clear my head."

His roar of laughter startled a flock of geese grazing on a nearby field. *He doesn't believe me.* "And landed in the ditch for a reward, did you? Oh well, must be off, the Board awaits."

The Board? Libby's brain seemed to whirr into action. Could her hunch be right? She tried to sound casual. "Is that the Board of Pritchards?"

Wendlebury's brows came together. For the first time, he seemed confused. "Ah. Well, one of the irons I like to keep in the fire, you know."

"I hear you're looking for premises around here." She kept her voice light.

"Now, m'dear. Let's not worry about business just now. I think you should be on your way home to have a nice mug of hot chocolate. I'd offer to make you some, myself, if I didn't have this meeting."

He made a show of looking at his watch. "Heavens, look at the time. Can't be late. Better get that car started, just to be sure."

He stepped towards Libby, but she opened the door and slipped into the driving seat, turning the key in the ignition as she went. The car coughed once and Libby drew a sharp breath. *Please, please, start.* The prayer worked. The engine turned over smoothly. She relaxed, wound down the window, smiled, waved and drove off.

As she drove, she glanced in the rear view mirror. Wendlebury peered after her for a long moment. Finally, he climbed into his own vehicle and drove in the opposite direction. Libby took her foot off the accelerator and pulled in to the side of the road. She needed to stop and take a breath.

As she slowed, she glanced in the mirror once more. What she saw made her gasp. The Range Rover was approaching fast from behind.

CHAPTER TWENTY-FOUR

Chase

Chesterton Wendlebury had turned round, and he was following Libby. She had to get home, fast. Every inch of her body was on high alert. She trod hard on the pedal and the car juddered as it gathered speed. *Don't break down, now.* The Citroen was small and nippy, taking bends in its stride. Libby kept her foot hard on the accelerator, ignoring the engine's anguished whine.

Soon the Range Rover fell back. Was Wendlebury letting her go, having lost the element of surprise? She wasn't waiting around to find out. There seemed to be no one else out on the Levels. Just as well. Libby, panic in her throat, would have run slap into any vehicle going the other way.

Was Chesterton Wendlebury trying to kill her? Could he be behind everything? Libby tried to think. Why would he have killed Kevin Batty?

The answer was obvious. Kevin had stopped his company from getting the land they wanted, and Wendlebury wasn't the kind of man to let anyone stand in his way. He'd never let go of a grudge. When Kevin stood up to Wendlebury, he signed his death warrant. Wendlebury, through Pritchards, had been working for years towards his revenge. No doubt he'd soon be approaching Kevin's family, trying to buy the land cheaply, now Kevin wasn't there to fight back.

Libby had asked about Steve. She shuddered, hands shaking on the wheel, stealing snatched glances through the mirror as the Range Rover slipped further behind. Her questions had put her on the list of people likely to stand in Wendlebury's way.

As she reached Exham, Libby shot one more glance in the mirror. The Range Rover had disappeared. Tears of relief filled her eyes. He'd given up.

There was her road. She screeched to a halt, jumped out of the car and ran into the house. She was safe, for now. Maybe Wendlebury's meeting was too important for him to waste time dealing with Libby, but it wouldn't be long before he found her again. There was nowhere in Exham to hide.

Shaking, Libby pulled out her phone to dial the police. Halfway through the number she stopped. What was she going to tell them? That she'd run into Chesterton Wendlebury, a pillar of the establishment, he'd helped her out of the ditch and now she was accusing him of wanting to kill her?

She cut off the dial tone. Joe, she knew, would support her if he could, but she needed hard evidence. Frank was still the likeliest suspect in police eyes. She sighed and pressed more buttons. She'd call Max.

"Hello, Libby. That was quite a day at the show." The warmth in his voice sent a rush of mixed emotions through Libby. A stomach-jangle and a smile she couldn't quite shake off, along with a flicker of guilt. Wendlebury had interrupted them at the show, preventing her responding properly to Max's confidences.

There was no time for that, now. She took a shuddering breath. "Max. I need your help, again."

His tone changed, sounded urgent. "What's wrong?"

"He's after me. Can you come?"

"Calm down. Is someone there?"

"No. But he's on his way."

"Who is? And where are you?"

"Wendlebury." She could hardly say the name through her chattering teeth. "Chesterton Wendlebury. He's coming after me. I'm at home."

"Wendlebury? Libby, what are you talking about?"

"Stop arguing. Just get here." A sigh travelled across the airwaves. Was he going to refuse to come? "Max, I need you."

"Okay, just lock the doors and stay inside. I'm on my way."

Libby checked the doors and windows, then checked them again. She held the phone in one hand, counting the bars that registered the strength of the signal, as she shivered with fear. How long would it take Max to arrive? Twenty minutes? Trembling, she watched the hand on the kitchen clock tick round.

Six minutes, then seven. Maybe, if Max drove fast he could do it in fifteen...

The doorbell rang. He'd arrived. He must have really put his foot down. Libby staggered to the front door and flung it open.

Simon Logan smiled. Libby, too relieved to be polite, gasped, "Simon? Whatever are you doing here?"

"Hello. Can I come in? I wanted to ask you something." Libby leaned against the wall, knees weak. Simon's brows drew together. "Are you OK?"

She beamed. She couldn't help it. He was tall, strong and handsome, and those warm brown eyes seemed to draw her in. "You've saved me." She bit her lip. "Someone's after me."

"After you? Who?"

"Chesterton Wendlebury. He killed Kevin Batty and tried to kill Steve. I'm next."

Simon stepped forward and hugged her. "Why, you're shaking. I'm sure you're imagining things." His voice was deep and very comforting. Libby leaned into his body. Gently, he took her shoulders and turned her round. "Let's go inside and sit down, and you can tell me all about it."

He followed Libby down the hall to the kitchen. She swallowed. "I'm sure he's the killer. He was following me and I only just managed to get away."

"You mean, he chased you in that Range Rover, and you lost him in your little Citroen? I don't think so." He laughed, his voice too loud, echoing through the cottage. Libby's heart lurched and she spun round. Simon was only inches away, one hand out of sight behind his back.

Startled, Libby took an awkward step backwards, tripped and stumbled across the room. Simon followed, his voice purring, menacing. "If he'd wanted to catch you, he would. You're not as sharp as you imagine, Mrs Forest."

She whispered, through dry lips. "It's not Wendlebury, is it?" So much suddenly fell into place. Meeting Simon at the picnic and handing over the sandwiches. Kevin Batty and his love of cars. Vince's heart condition. Angela's husband and the accident...

Simon's smile was cold, now, those brown eyes suddenly as hard as stones. "Not Wendlebury, no."

Libby could hardly get the words out. "It was you, all the time."

Simon's left arm was still hidden behind his back. His right hand shot out and grabbed the neck of Libby's sweater, pulling her face close. "You've been interfering a little too much, Mrs Forest. All that talk of manuscripts and sprained wrists. You knew I'd written that music, not Geoff, didn't you?"

"N-no. I didn't realise..." Music? What was he talking about?

"All those questions you've been asking at the garage, about Kevin Batty. You've been after me for days."

"What do you mean? I wasn't..."

"Don't pretend. You've talked to them all. Alan Jenkins, Steve, Angela."

She had to keep him talking. "Angela? What does she have to do with it?"

He sneered. "Don't try to pretend you don't know about Geoff and me. It was all in the past. Forgotten. Water under the bridge. I thought I was safe. Then, Kevin spoiled everything."

"How? What happened?"

"One night, we were in the Lighthouse Inn. Alan, Kevin and me. Kevin started talking about the old days, when they used to fix cars together. Alan mentioned Geoff Miles's Porsche and the crash. He said he'd been afraid he'd get the blame for Geoff's death, because one of the nuts on a wheel was loose. He said it was Geoff's own fault. He'd always been a crazy driver."

Frantic, unable to move her head, Libby peered from side to side, searching for something to grab, anything she could use to disable Simon.

He thrust his face closer, spit flying from his lips. "Kevin was cleverer than people thought. He looked at me, while Alan was talking, and I saw the light dawn in that ugly rat-face. Next day, he rang me, offering to forget all about it for half a million quid." Simon's lip twisted. "The fool. Always after money. He found out he was messing with the wrong man."

Libby had to keep him talking. Simon needed to tell her how clever he'd been. Her only chance was to play along and hope Max would arrive in time. Simon's hand gripped tight round her throat, crushing her windpipe, his body pushing her hard against the wall. She croaked, "You killed Geoff? But why?"

"He double-crossed me. He stole my work. We were mates, both struggling to make a living in music. I was making twice as much as him, writing advertising jingles." Fury distorted Simon Logan's face. "He had a mental block. He was stuck. Couldn't write a note more of his quintet, the one he thought would take the music world by storm. Like a fool, I helped him out. He swore he'd share the credit." His hands were so tight, Libby's head swam. Her breath came in short gasps. If Max didn't arrive soon, it would be too late.

Simon's eyes were glassy. "Nothing happened with Geoff's work for years. No one cared. Then, suddenly he was offered film work. Before long, he was famous, his stuff played everywhere. He toured Europe and the USA, and then, like a magician, he produced that long-lost quintet. The critics loved it and he lapped up the praise. He never mentioned my name. Not once. I couldn't prove I'd written it. Who would have believed me? He was the maestro! He let me perform in it, like he was doing me a favour."

Tears streaked down Simon's face. His voice shook. "We were friends and he cheated me. He'd already stolen Angela. He deserved to die." Madness shone in his eyes. "And so do you."

The doorbell rang. Libby screamed. "Max!"

"He's too late." Simon was laughing. The doorbell kept on ringing. Max hammered on the door. *The door's too solid. He'll never break it down.*

175

Still throttling Libby with one hand, Simon brought his right arm round from behind his back. Something glinted in the light and Libby tensed for the blow.

"Stop!" The shriek came from the doorway that led to the hall.

From the corner of her eye, Libby caught sight of Mandy. "Stay there," she gasped, but Mandy ran, screaming like a banshee, grabbed Simon's arm, and twisted it round behind his back. With one hand still grasping Libby's throat, he couldn't throw Mandy off. The syringe fell and shattered on the floor. Simon swore and his grip on Libby's throat loosened.

She grabbed the sleeve of his jacket. With all her strength, Libby held on. Simon raised his free arm to strike her but Mandy was back, the chocolate grinder in her hands.

With a crash, she brought it down on Simon's head. He fell, heavily, awkwardly, cracking his face against Libby's cherished marble floor tiles, and lay still.

Mandy and Libby looked at each other, aghast. The glass in the kitchen door shattered, and Max's face appeared. Hysteria began to bubble up inside Libby. "You're too late," she croaked, and slid to the floor. Mandy ran to the kitchen door and let Max in.

"It looks as though you've managed perfectly well without me," Max complained. Libby sat with her back propped against the wall, grinning like an idiot.

Max checked Simon was still breathing and rang 999. "Your efficiency is not at all good for my ego. We should tie him up, though, just in case."

Libby scrambled to her feet, searched in the drawers, and pulled out a handful of plastic ties. Max took them. "Perfect." He clipped Simon's wrists together behind his back.

"Not too tight," Libby said. Max looked from her to Simon, smiled and pulled the plastic tie a notch tighter.

Libby scrambled to her feet and hugged Mandy. "I'd forgotten you were in the house."

"I was asleep for hours. Then Aunt Angela sent me a text. Look." She tilted her phone so Libby could see. *Steve awake. On the mend. He'd love to see you.* "I was just about to ring for a taxi when I heard Max at the door."

If Angela hadn't texted Mandy, she would still be asleep. Libby would have died. "Mandy, you're wonderful."

The girl's smile threatened to split her face in two. Minus makeup, cheeks aglow with excitement, she frowned. "But what was Simon Logan doing, attacking you?"

Max pointed to a broken syringe on the floor. "I imagine the police will find that's full of digitalis."

CHAPTER TWENTY-FIVE

Orange drizzle cake

Joe arrived with Constable Ian Smith in tow, as Simon began to rouse, twitching and cursing. Ian Smith rammed a pair of handcuffs on the man's wrists. "Though, to be honest, Mrs Forest, your plastic ties work just as well."

Simon squirmed, face twisted with fury, lips curled in a snarl. Every sign of the courteous gentleman act had vanished. Constable Smith dragged him to his feet and shoved him into the police car. "We'll need statements from each of you," Joe said, "but they can wait. I want to hear what Mr Logan has to say for himself, first."

Max had an arm round Libby. She didn't object, for her legs felt distinctly wobbly. Max still seemed confused. "I don't understand much of this. Why did Simon Logan poison Kevin and Vince, and try to kill Steve and Libby? None of it makes sense."

Libby's brain raced as pieces fell into place. "I think I can see some of it," she said, "but we need to talk to Angela. She's involved."

Mandy's hand flew to her mouth. "I forgot. She sent another text. She's going to the local history society meeting and she told me to ask you to bring the cakes."

Libby laughed. "Cakes. Just what we all need. Max, I bet you've never set foot in a local history meeting."

"I'm game for anything. Let's go."

***

The meeting was in full swing as they arrived at Marina's house. "Darling," she cried. "Thank goodness you've arrived. We're all dying for cake. We'd given up on you and I was just about to break out some old custard creams, instead."

They trooped into the beautifully elegant drawing room. Chesterton Wendlebury's bulk spread over both seats of a two-seater chesterfield. "Mrs Forest," he said, "I'm so glad to see you. After our little incident, I realised I had my days quite mixed up and my meeting isn't until tomorrow. So I turned around and followed you into town. I must say, dear lady, you're impossible to catch on the road. I never knew a little Citroen like that could travel so fast."

Libby's cheeks burned. Did the man have any idea she'd been racing to get away from him? That twinkle in his eyes made her wonder. She let Marina take the orange drizzle cake, slide it onto the waiting plate and hand it round, neatly sliced. Marina wriggled into the space next to Chesterton. Libby glanced at Angela, who raised an eyebrow. Had no one else noticed how often those two were together?

In the corner of the room, the society's longest-serving member, Beryl, flicked through a sheaf of papers. Libby's heart sank. Beryl was planning to give her long-anticipated talk on the history of the post office, and there was only one way to escape it. "We thought you'd want to know we've discovered who poisoned Kevin Batty and Vince Lane, and tried to kill Angela's nephew, Steve."

In the hubbub of gasps, guesses and questions that greeted the announcement, Beryl gave a weary sigh, folded her notes and slid them into a battered brown handbag, snapping the bag shut with a click.

Marina raised her vigorous contralto above the rest. "Come on, Libby. Stop milking it and tell us."

"It was Simon Logan." As the noise died down, Libby explained. "I was very stupid. You see, because two members of the cycle club died and several others were taken ill, it was easy to think the poison was meant for everyone. In fact, Kevin Batty was the only intended victim."

Libby watched her audience. Each face betrayed surprise, excitement, confusion, or a mix of all three. "Simon was very clever. He'd brought digitoxin, ready for Kevin, to the picnic, but when I delivered the sandwiches that day, he saw a chance to cover his tracks. He took all the food from me."

It was embarrassing. Annoyed with Max for keeping secrets, for not trusting her, she'd been easily flattered by Simon's attention. He'd rushed over as soon as she arrived, but he hadn't been at all interested in Libby. He was just keen to get his hands on the food.

Libby kept her face turned away from Max. "Simon had plenty of time to add poison to the food. Just a little in a sandwich here, or a cake there, so that most people swallowed some."

She thought back to the scene at the water's edge. It had looked so innocent. "Simon wanted to make sure Kevin died. Poisoning the food wasn't enough. Simon injected poison straight into Kevin."

Angela asked. "Wouldn't the police pathologist find marks from the syringe?"

"I puzzled over that, too. Alan Jenkins had given me the answer, quite by chance. When I was in the garage, Alan grazed his hand. He told me it happened all the time. His hands are always covered with cuts and scrapes and Kevin's were, too. He loved tinkering with custom cars, like Alan.

"All Simon had to do was wait until the first effects of the digitoxin in the food made Kevin ill. While he was nauseous and woozy, Simon injected him with a full dose, positioning the needle on the site of an old graze. One little needle mark would be almost impossible to find, among the scratches on Kevin's hand. Simon was a cool customer."

Marina frowned. "I suppose he had a mouthful or too of the poisoned food. Just enough to make himself ill. No one suspected him, at all. I can understand how he made sure Kevin died, but why Vince?"

"I was puzzled by that, as well, until I met Vince's neighbour. He told me Vince had a heart condition and took medication. I bet Vince's medical records show the doctor prescribed a form of digitalis to keep his heart regular. The dose from the sandwiches, combined with his regular tablets, gave him a fatal overdose. Vince's death was just an accident."

Libby suddenly remembered something else Vince's neighbour had said. "Members of the club used to visit Vince, when he first had trouble with his heart. Simon must have been in the house. He could have gone to the bathroom, found Vince's medication and helped himself to some. He wouldn't have to go to the trouble of collecting foxglove leaves. All he had to do was crush Vince's tablets and dissolve them."

Angela shivered. "You've told us how he managed it, but not the reason. Why did Simon Logan kill Kevin Batty?"

"It goes back ten years, I'm afraid, to the day your husband died."

Angela gasped, her face suddenly pale. "I'm sorry," Libby said. "No one suspected foul play when Geoff crashed his car, because he was driving far too fast"

"That's true," Angela whispered.

"Simon Logan had loosened a wheel nut on Geoff's car, making it steer all over the road, knowing Geoff would eventually go too fast and crash off the road. He could have tampered with the car any time. Maybe several days before the crash. All he had to do was wait. No wonder he was certain he'd got away with it."

Angela's knuckles were pressed to her face. Libby swept on, keen to finish the story. "One day, Simon was in the Lighthouse Inn with Kevin and Alan, and they got talking about the old days and their favourite subject, cars. Alan mentioned the loose wheel nut on Geoff's Porsche. Simon Logan was shocked. After all, the murder had been unsuspected for ten years. Kevin saw the look on Simon's face and jumped to the right conclusion. Unfortunately for Kevin, he tried a spot of blackmail. I imagine Simon played along, maybe even made a payment or two, all the while plotting to kill Kevin."

Max put in, "We all know Kevin was brighter than people gave him credit for, and he loved money."

Angela was shaking her head slowly, dazed. "I don't understand. Why would Simon want to kill Geoff? They were friends. At one time, I thought they'd be partners, but then Simon went off to make money from his jingles. Why did Simon hate my husband?"

CHAPTER TWENTY-SIX

Back in business

If only Libby didn't have to tell the whole tale. She'd give anything to leave matters there, but Angela deserved the truth. Libby sighed, and let the words tumble out. "Simon killed Geoff out of jealousy, partly because you married him instead of Simon." Angela flushed scarlet.

Libby braced herself to deliver the final blow that was going to break her friend's heart. "Simon did nothing about it. They stayed friends. After all, Simon's career was solid, while Geoff had yet to make his mark in the world. He was even willing to help his old friend out. But then, Geoff double-crossed Simon and stole his work, and that was the last straw."

All the colour drained from Angela's face. "Stole his work? What do you mean?"

"You remember the different style of writing on the last few pages of Geoff's manuscript? It was nothing to do with a sprained wrist, or tiredness, or anything like that. It was Simon's writing. He composed the music. Geoff had a mental block and he couldn't finish the quintet, so his friend did it for him."

Angela walked over to the window, to gaze out towards the smooth green knoll behind the house. Her words were strangled when she spoke, as though her throat had constricted. "It's true Geoff was having a few problems. He told me once he thought his creativity was drying up, but then he seemed to get over it. If only I'd realised he was struggling." She twisted the cord of her glasses, tying it in knots. "I never realised. Oh, Geoff, why didn't you tell me?"

Libby said, "He asked his old friend to help him out. Then, by the time he was famous, he didn't think it mattered that the work wasn't his own."

Angela scrubbed at her eyes, the ball of tissue close to disintegration. "I knew Geoff could be selfish. His work always came first, but I would never have believed he'd let his friend down, like that. How could he be so dishonest?"

Marina heaved herself off the sofa to offer Angela an expensive, scented handkerchief. "And the attempt on Steve?"

Libby remembered the scene at the rehearsal. Friends, enjoying the sun on the patio. Mandy getting her rival drunk, Simon explaining how Geoff always drove too fast. "Steve was there when we talked about the manuscript. How the writing was different from Geoff's. Simon told me about Geoff's accident. He must have been trying to put me off the scent. I was getting too close, asking about Kevin and then talking about the manuscript."

Her shoulders sagged. "I suppose that was when he decided he had to get rid of me, but first he had to deal with Steve, who remembered Geoff's accident so clearly. One day, Steve might put two and two together, like Kevin did. It must have been easy, driving up close behind Steve, forcing his motor bike off the road. The police will find the scrapings of paint on Steve's bike match Simon's car.

"Then, Simon came to finish the job and kill me. He would have succeeded, too, but for Mandy. She's the real hero of the day."

Angela's damp smile wavered, but she said, "Mandy's quite a girl, even if she does her best to put everyone off with those awful tattoos."

Libby opened her mouth, then closed it again. No need to tell anyone her suspicion that Mandy's tattoos were fake. The girl was entitled to a little deception.

Libby's phone rang. She slid it out of her pocket and pressed the green button. "Mandy? Is everything OK?"

"More than that. Frank's out of jail, and the bakery's opening again tomorrow. Frank says, please bring plenty of chocolates, because he's contacted the press and they'll all be there in the morning."

***

Ali rang, that evening. She gave a blow by blow account of the journey to South America, complete with love-struck declarations of Andy's kindness, cleverness and street-wisdom. As her phone battery was dying, she asked, "Anything exciting happened in Exham, Mum? Did you solve the great food-poisoning mystery?"

Libby took a deep breath. No point getting Ali in a flap, not when she was on the other side of the world. "It's all sorted out. Fuzzy and I are having a quiet evening. Enjoy yourself."

It was late, by the time Libby put the finishing touches to the batch of chocolates. Proud, she counted the trays and the pile of cardboard ballotins. Tomorrow, they'd be on sale at the bakery. Every single member of the local history society had put in a huge advance order.

Max had brought her home after the meeting, trying to persuade her to get an early night and promising to meet next morning, to walk Shipley and Bear on the beach.

Libby waved him off, glad they were friends again. However maddening the man could be, she knew she could turn to him whenever she needed help.

Friendship was quite enough, for now. She was ashamed to think how quickly she'd succumbed to Simon Logan's false charms. So much for her proud boast of independence. Her powers of intuition obviously needed a reboot if she wasn't to fall for every attractive killer she met.

The cat stretched out on the sofa, catching the last rays of sun. Libby poured a glass of wine, curled up beside Fuzzy and stroked the soft head. For once, the cat let her.

Who knew what would become of Max and Libby in the months to come? He was still investigating AJP Associates. Pritchards were innocent of Kevin's murder, but they were still in Max's sights for fraud and money laundering, and he'd be off on his travels again soon, gathering evidence. At least he'd promised to leave Bear with Libby in future.

Libby still had to get to the bottom of Trevor's involvement. Maybe tomorrow she'd think about it. There were still loose ends to be tied up, like Trevor's strange instruction not to sell the house for five years.

Tonight, it didn't seem to matter. Libby sighed, contented, pleased that Mandy would be back soon, from another visit to Steve. For the first time, Libby felt at home in Exham. She buried her face in the cat's warm fur. "I think we'll stay here a while longer, Fuzzy."

Thank you for reading Murder on the Levels. I hope you had fun with the inhabitants of Exham on Sea. If you enjoyed the story, please tell other readers by adding a short review on Amazon.

About the author…

Frances Evesham writes mystery stories: the Exham on Sea contemporary crime series set in a small Somerset seaside town, and the Thatcham Hall Mysteries, 19th Century historical mystery romances set in Victorian England.

She collects grandsons, Victorian ancestors and historical trivia, likes to smell the roses, lavender and rosemary, and cooks with a glass of wine in one hand and a bunch of chillies in the other. She loves the Arctic Circle and the equator and plans to visit the penguins in the south one day.

She's been a speech therapist, a professional communicator and a road sweeper and worked in the criminal courts. Now, she walks in the country and breathes sea air in Somerset.

Find out more online at:
www.franceshevesham.com
www.twitter.com/franceshevesham
www.facebook.com/frances.evesham.writer

If you enjoyed Murder on the Levels, you may like Murder on the Tor, the third Exham on Sea Mystery.

More cosy crime, murder mysteries, clever animals, cake, and chocolate all feature in the second Exham on Sea mystery, set in a seaside town in Somerset.

When two cyclists die on the remote Somerset Levels, the Exham bakery gets the blame. Libby Forest runs into danger as she sets out to solve the mystery, save the bakery and rescue her career, helped by Bear, the enormous Carpathian Sheepdog, Fuzzy, an aloof marmalade cat and the handsome, secretive Max Ramshore.

The Exham on Sea Mystery stories feature a cast of local characters, including Mandy the teenage Goth, Frank the baker and Detective Sergeant Joe Ramshore, Max's estranged son. The green fields, rolling hills and sandy beaches of the West Country provide the perfect setting for crime, intrigue and mystery.

For lovers of Agatha Christie novels, Midsomer Murders, lovable pets and cake, the series offers a continuing supply of quick crime stories, each one short enough to read in one sitting.

**The Exham on Sea Mysteries:
Contemporary Cosy Crime Fiction**
Murder at the Lighthouse
Murder on the Levels
Murder on the Tor

**The Thatcham Hall Mysteries:
Victorian Fiction**
An Independent Woman
Danger at Thatcham Hall

**Free Kindle Ebook:
True Crime**
Murder Most Victorian: available from
www.francesevesham.com/murder-most-victorian

The characters and events described in the Exham on Sea Mysteries are all entirely fictitious. Some landmarks may strike fellow residents of Somerset, and particularly of Burnham on Sea, as familiar, although I've taken some liberties with a few locations.

Made in the USA
Middletown, DE
12 November 2018